9/24

VALERON'S RANGE

When Scarlet Valeron, poised to be married in Pueblo, Colorado, is kidnapped and her betrothed killed, a desperate call goes out to the Valeron family. Brothers, cousins, and hired help unite in an effort to find her and bring her back. They learn Scarlet is on her way to Brimstone, a bandit stronghold of over a hundred outlaws. Most would look at the incredible odds and figure Scarlet was lost forever. The Valerons, however, see it as a matter of family honour to get their kin back, and settle the score!

TERRELL L. BOWERS

VALERON'S
RANGE

Complete and Unabridged

LINFORD
Leicester

First published in Great Britain in 2016 by
Robert Hale
an imprint of The Crowood Press
Wiltshire

First Linford Edition
published 2019
by arrangement with
The Crowood Press
Wiltshire

A catalogue record for this book is available
from the British Library.

ISBN 978–1–4448–4235–7

Published by
F. A. Thorpe (Publishing)
Anstey, Leicestershire

Set by Words & Graphics Ltd.
Anstey, Leicestershire
Printed and bound in Great Britain by
T. J. International Ltd., Padstow, Cornwall

This book is printed on acid-free paper

1

Maria turned from her chores to push Cliff away. She angrily shook her head. 'Stop it! I am not going to be your plaything.'

Flashing his dazzling smile, Cliff Mason attempted to nuzzle her neck once more. 'Come on, sweetness,' he whispered. 'The king and queen aren't home. No one is going to know.'

'Mrs Valeron said you weren't to be in the house.'

'Aw, my mother always said Aunt Wanetta is a mother hen, always sticking her beak in where it don't belong.'

'What happened between you and Veta?' she enquired. 'I thought you were panting after her?'

'Man wasn't made to love just one woman,' he replied. 'Remember Solomon?'

'He was a king . . . you are a lecher.'

'How can you say that?' He was not

dissuaded. 'You haven't given me a chance.'

Maria grunted her distrust. 'Shane warned me that you were a real hound.'

'Cousin Shane is a puritan and about as exciting as a church social. I don't know what you see in him.'

'He's a gentleman for one thing,' she defended the youngest Valeron boy in the three families. 'A girl can go for a walk with him and no one thinks she is risking her virtue.'

'All right, I give up.' But he still reached out to tug on her arm. 'Come with me. I've got a surprise for you. It'll be fun . . . and I'll be good.'

'Good is not a word I've ever heard associated with you.'

'No, Maria. I mean it. There's a new foal out at the barn — durned near as cute as you. It's past his feeding time and the mare doesn't have any milk. I promised Shane I would bottle-feed him.'

Maria frowned in thought. 'I would like to feed the colt . . .' She waggled a cautionary finger at him. ' . . . but that's all.'

'Sure, sure,' he agreed. 'Let's get out there before it gets dark.'

Maria consented and Cliff took her by the hand. They went through the house, but paused at the back porch to pick up two nipped-bottles that had been filled with cow's milk. Then they made their way over to the enormous barn that sat some distance beyond the principal Valeron home.

The colt was only two weeks old and eager for his feeding. Before Maria could get the bottle to the gate, he was pawing and pushing at the fence with his nose. He drank the milk with a furious gusto, sucking, pulling and tugging on the rubber nipple, while bobbing his head and happily swishing his tail. His enthusiasm caused Maria to laugh.

'Didn't I tell you?' Cliff murmured, slipping up behind her, leaning forward until his breath was on the back of her neck. 'No hands. No touching . . . yet.'

Maria suddenly let go of the bottle

and jumped to the side. Before Cliff could determine what was up, a wall of water came down from the loft. Two full pails right on Cliff's head and shoulders.

'Hey!' he cried, staggering back from the stall, soaking wet. 'What the hell?'

'That ought to cool some of those burning embers of passion,' Jared Valeron called down. 'I promised Mom that we'd see you didn't bother the help while she was away.'

'Time you learned some manners, cousin,' Shane Valeron joined in. 'My mother also has some concerns about your alley-cat ways.'

'You guys!' Cliff cried, wiping off the excess water. 'Feeding the foal was a set-up. I — '

But something small and hard exploded against the back of his head. He whirled about to see what had hit him and a second egg splatted against his forehead.

'That's a present from me!' Veta shouted, having been hidden in one of the stalls. 'Next time you want a kiss, try one of the mules!'

'Be sure to lift his tail first!' Shane jeered. 'Even a mule wouldn't let you kiss him on the lips!'

'Ah, man!' Cliff whined, trying to remove the egg from his face and hair. 'Did everyone on the entire ranch gang up on me?'

Veta strode over and kicked him smartly in the shin. He let out a yelp, cut off in mid-cry, as she gave him a push. Off balance, he sat down hard on the straw-littered barn floor.

Maria picked up the second bottle of milk and returned to feeding the colt. Shane and Jared climbed down from the loft, still snickering about Cliff's discomfort and humiliation.

Cliff rubbed his shin with one hand and continued to comb egg out of his long locks of blond hair with the other. He seldom wore a hat when at the house, being too vain to hide his golden head of hair. It, along with his ice-blue eyes, set him off as the best looking guy on the Valeron spread. Locke and Temple Valeron's kids all had the same rather average brown hair and eyes. As for the third brother, Udall, his children were a bit more fair. The girls were pretty, but the three boys were quite plain. Cliff took every advantage of being handsome.

'I owe you guys,' he avowed to Jared. 'Just wait — I'll get you back.'

Jared grinned at his threat. 'This was payment for constantly trying to charm the pants off our domestic help. Mom and Aunt Gwen have been complaining about you. Even Aunt Faye is fed up with your snorting around every hired girl like a bull at the first green of spring.'

'I only offer them a special peek at heaven.' Cliff sniffed piously. 'Can I help it if I'm irresistible to women?'

Jared winked at Shane. 'Cliff needs help cleaning off the dirt and eggs. What do you think?'

'I've got south,' Shane said, grabbing his feet.

'And I've got north,' Jared replied,

taking hold under Cliff's arms.

'Hey! No!' Cliff cried, trying to twist and buck his way loose.

It was no use. The next freedom for Cliff was when he splashed down in the watering trough. He was still cursing as Jared, Shane, and the two girls started to return to the house. The laughter pretty much drowned out his oaths and dire warnings of retribution.

A rider coming at full-tilt stopped the small procession, as well as Cliff's wailing. It was Wyatt Valeron, Udall's eldest son. He had been in town for the past few days.

'Trouble!' he shouted. 'Gather everyone at the main house.'

As it was dusk, most of the family members were at home for the day. Shane went to his house, and Maria hurried off to fetch Udall's family. Jared entered the primary home and discovered his brother, Reese, had arrived while he had been at the barn. With Locke, his wife and one daughter gone to attend their sister's wedding, there was only the two of them staying at the main house.

After putting away his horse, Wyatt came in to join Jared and Reese. Another of Locke's sons, Brett, was a U.S. Marshal and off on a job. Nash, the fourth son in the family, seldom visited the ranch since he had decided to become a doctor. Temple's kids were Troy, Shane, Darcy, Tish, and their oldest girl, Lana, was married. She and her husband had a house in town. As for Udall's household, him and his wife, plus his oldest boy, Martin and his wife arrived. Wyatt didn't live on the ranch, and Udall's other son, Fargo, often stayed at the housing at the Valeron coal mine. Cliff, still soaked from his unplanned bath, represented Udall's brother-in-law, who lived near Denver with their own family.

'All right.' Udall took charge, being the senior member of the family present. 'As you all know, Locke and Temple are in Pueblo to attend Scarlet's wedding, while me and Faye remained here to watch over the ranch. Something has happened and they sent us a wire.' He nodded at his son. 'Wyatt happened to be in town and brought this telegraph message home.'

'It's bad news.' Wyatt didn't keep them in suspense. 'Scarlet has been kidnapped.' He allowed that to sink in before continuing. 'Several men entered the Logan house and took Scarlet by force. Fred's parents were knocked unconscious. Fred put up more of a fight and was killed.'

Everyone knew not to burst out with questions. They waited while Wyatt outlined what was to be done. 'Locke has instructed three of us to begin the search for Scarlet. He will send us a second wire in the morning telling us anything they can learn about the kidnapping.'

'When do we leave?' Jared wanted to know. 'Them dirty low-down snakes are gonna pay with their lives for this!'

'I'm going, too, Uncle Udall,' Cliff said firmly. 'I got a right to help find my cousin.'

Udall grimaced. 'I'd rather have your

brother, Rod. He's as capable as any of the Valeron boys.'

'Yeah,' Cliff quipped, 'but he ain't here. I am.'

Udall argued no further. He turned back to Wyatt. 'What is Locke's plan?'

'Jared,' Wyatt outlined, 'your pa wants you, because you are the best hunter or tracker around. And Shane,' he turned his attention to him, 'we need you because you're a top hand with horseflesh. He naturally chose me, being that I'm better with a gun than anyone else on the ranch.'

'And I make four of us,' Cliff announced.

'Don't know if any of the kidnappers are women,' Wyatt told him. 'So I'm not sure how much help you'll be. However,' he added, raising his hands to stop any objection, 'taking you along would give the girls working on the ranch a few days' relief from your constant harassment.'

Cliff grinned. 'See? Either way it's a win.'

'Round up the supplies and anything

else you need,' Wyatt outlined. 'Shane, let's take a couple extra horses. We'll need to carry water when we cross the desert areas, and we can switch our mounts to rest a horse or two each day.'

'We'll need to have an extra if one comes up lame, too,' Shane replied. 'I'll have the best steeds available and ready to ride by first light.'

'Just you four?' Udall wondered. 'Do we even know how many attackers there are?'

'Numbers don't matter,' Jared declared. 'Every man-jack involved is a walking corpse!'

Wyatt ignored Jared's outburst. 'Several attackers were mentioned in the wire. Locke and Temple promised to send what information they could get by the time we reach town tomorrow morning. I imagine they will have a few chores lined out for some of the rest of you by then.'

'I'll ride in with you and bring back any instructions for the rest of us,' Martin offered.

'I made some cookies today,' Darcy, one of Temple's daughters, volunteered. 'You can take some of them with you.'

'Unless they turn out like oatmeal stone lumps again,' Tish teased her older sister.

'Then they can use them in case they need something hard to throw!' Darcy quipped back. 'Save looking around for rocks.'

Udall's wife interjected, 'There's twenty pounds of venison jerky hanging in the smokehouse. Everyone pick up a supply before you leave.'

'Too bad Cliff washed his hair.' Shane smirked. 'We could have had eggs along the trail.'

'I'll get you a couple to stick in your pockets before we pull out,' Cliff shot back.

Wyatt held up a hand for silence. Humor was a dominant trait in the Valeron clan. Fate had often dealt serious or even fatal blows to several members of this sizable family, but they never lost their zest for life or allowed negative emotions to dictate their actions.

Witticism gave them strength, resilience and positive reinforcement. He didn't criticize the levity, but he was unable to hide the angst he felt concerning the seriousness of this endeavor.

'OK,' he remained sedate, 'one of our family members is out there, alone and frightened. Scarlet knows we'll come after her, so let's not keep her waiting any longer than necessary.'

The group broke up, each going to their own house. Cliff, who bunked with the hired hands, remained in the main house. Once everyone had left except Jared and Reese, he spoke up.

'If it's all right with you two, I'll bring my stuff over and bunk here tonight.' He flashed a smirk. 'Wouldn't want you forgetting about me and leaving me behind.'

'You're welcome to stay,' Reese allowed. Then he frowned. 'How come you're all wet?'

'Jared and Shane ganged up on me,' Cliff complained. 'You being the eldest of the Valeron boys means you should have taught your kin how to behave.'

Reese grinned. 'If I'd have been here, I'd have joined in on the fun. A good lesson now might save your life down the road. One day, you'll latch on to the wrong heifer and some he-bull will stomp his spurs right through your breastbone.'

'Fine thing,' Cliff whined. 'I do my bit to keep up morale on this ranch and all I catch is shrapnel from the bunch of you.'

'You are more interested in keeping up *immoral* behavior on the ranch,' Jared countered. 'There's a big difference.'

'Well, I'm glad of one thing.' Cliff snorted. 'At least my last name ain't Valeron!'

'Amen to that,' Reese said meaningfully. 'Amen to that.'

★   ★   ★

Brett Valeron had finished a three-week manhunt. Red Dog Cutter and his two Indian pals had been drinking whiskey and gone to sleep around a small campfire. They awoke to find their weapons

14

confiscated and staring down the muzzle of Brett's gun. Six hours later, they were at the jail in Julesburg, awaiting trial for robbery and murder. Now he was relaxing on the train, heading home and looking idly out of the passenger car window and watching the scenery go by.

Well, there was one other bit of scenery that had caught his eye. A young lady, who looked to be in her early twenties, petite in build, maybe an inch or two over five feet. Modestly dressed, she wore a Quaker-style bonnet that hid most of her extraordinarily colored hair. She had been in the family car, but came and went through the second car, which was for immigrants and single men traveling. As there were a number of available seats on this particular train, most of the passengers took advantage of being able to walk about from one to the other for exercise.

The thing that stuck in Brett's mind was the coy, yet scrutinizing way the girl kept watching two particular men. One was dressed like a banker, attired in an expensive suit and a businessman's hat. He was a talkative sort and had attempted to chat to several of the people from the emigrant car. From the bits of conversation Brett overheard, he deduced the gent was trying to sell parcels of land to some of the pilgrim families. The second man was clothed like a farmer, but when he passed by closely, Brett took note of his soft, smooth hands — nothing like the gnarled and callused hands of a man who worked the soil. He suspected he was a gambler or salesman and mentally tagged the pair with suitable epithets: Banker and Gambler. The two pretended only a passing acquaintance, but Brett saw them exchange glances with one another to convey silent messages back and forth.

A couple of hustlers, he concluded. But why was the girl so interested?

It wasn't long before the two men found a sucker. English was not the fellow's first language, but he understood enough to be swayed by the two men. They offered to show him some deeds and moved to the baggage car for privacy. Brett kept his hat tipped down over his eyes enough to make it appear as if he was napping. The trio passed by without giving him a second look.

No sooner had the men left the immigrant car than the young lady came striding past. She had been trying to eavesdrop, but was now on the wrong rail-car. Even as she stepped through the door, an unobtrusive man rose from his seat. He walked with deliberation, trailing behind the girl.

Brett stretched and yawned, taking a clandestine peek at the man. Mean-faced, with a scar over one eye and a nose that looked to have been broken more than once, he had the hands of a fighter. He moved with purpose and a cruel set to his jaw.

When he exited the car, Brett hurried after him. He opened the door just in time to see the big guy grab the girl. She cried out and began to struggle, but his size dominated her efforts. Even as Brett started forward, the brute whirled the lady about, preparing to toss her off the train!

'I wouldn't!' Brett barked, aiming his Colt Peacemaker at the assailant. 'If you harm one hair on the lady's head, I'll kill you where you stand!'

The man relaxed his hold, allowing the girl to escape his grasp. Eyes fixed on the gun in Brett's hand, he slowly lifted his hands.

'Let's go inside the next car so we can sort this out,' Brett ordered. 'You too, ma'am.'

The woman moved over and opened the door. She stood off to one side while her attacker entered the car. The other three men were stunned to discover they were under the muzzle of a gun.

'I'm a U.S. Marshal,' Brett announced. 'And the game is up.'

'We're doing nothing illegal,' Banker replied quickly. 'I represent the Fremont Bank and Holding company. I have deeds to several parcels of land. Good land.'

'That's right,' Gambler confirmed quickly. 'I bought a parcel a few months back. I was merely vouching for this man.'

'They are swindlers!' the girl spoke up for the first time. 'The parcels of land they offer is barren desert property with no value whatsoever.'

Brett cast a sidelong glance at her, then turned back to Banker. 'Show me a deed and point out on a map where this land is,' he directed him.

The gent pulled a hand-drawn map from his pocket and opened it up. 'These are the parcels I have for sale. Every one is prime farmland.'

Brett was familiar with the location and grunted his disgust. 'Farmland . . . if you're raising scorpions, tumble-weeds or a passel of Indian kids. These plots of land have no access to water and are on the edge of the Wind River Indian reservation.'

'Vot?' the immigrant cried. 'I doan' vant no land vere dere be Indians!'

'You can go, mister,' Brett told the

would-be buyer. 'You other three are under arrest.'

'Hey! I only bought a parcel of land!' complained Gambler.

Brett ignored his objection. 'Empty your pockets and discard any weapons. You try anything and I'll see you get your own parcel of land . . . in the next cemetery we come to!'

As they began to do as they were told, Brett sent the lady to fetch the conductor. A few minutes later, the three men were locked in the same car as Brett's horse. He and the girl returned to the family car before she confronted him.

'What made you follow after me?'

'I noticed you keeping an eye on the two crooks.'

'You didn't need to get involved,' she said stiffly. 'I almost had my gun in hand. I wouldn't have allowed that big oaf to throw me off the train.'

Brett raised a single eyebrow. 'From my viewpoint, you were a trifle overmatched.'

The girl was still miffed. 'But you

made the arrest! I've been watching those two men for over a week. I almost had them at Kansas City, but they couldn't find a buyer.'

'What's your story, miss?' he asked. 'Who do you work for?'

'Al Pinkerton,' she announced with little amount of pride. 'Usually, I only have to watch for gamblers, out to fleece the immigrants, or a conductor who is selling rides without tickets. This time, there were complaints of someone duping settlers and selling them worthless homesteads. We had no other agents in the area, so I volunteered.'

Brett took notice that the girl was more attractive close up. She had apparently worked to hide her comely features in order to not attract attention. She had a pink flesh-tone, and hair that was rare indeed, closer to copper than red or auburn. The eyes were a dark green and her sensuous mouth —

'Excuse me,' she interrupted his assessment. 'It's quite rude to count the teeth of someone you just met. I'm not a horse for sale!'

Brett chuckled. 'Sorry for eying you like a pink and blue rooster, little lady. It's just that I've never come across a gal with your color of hair. Was your mother a redhead?'

His line of conversation deflated some of the billow from her defensive sails. With a sigh of patience, she answered, 'My father is Irish and my mother hailed from Sweden. She was blonde and he had rusty-colored hair. I suppose I got a little color from each of them.'

'Again, my apology for staring.' He offered her his best smile.

'You don't seem surprised that I am working for the Pinkerton agency.'

'I guessed it might be something along those lines. You are pretty good at spying on a subject, but that third man was a surprise. I never saw either of the other men make eye contact with him.'

'Nor did I,' she admitted candidly. 'They gave no indication of a third accomplice.'

'Smart hombres. Hire a brute to take care of an irate customer or some snoopy conductor. He could intervene if there was trouble and the other two would make their escape. Afterward, he could pretend ignorance. Be tough to pin anything on him other than disturbing the peace.'

'I should thank you for your help,' she said with some reluctance.

'Tell me,' he said. 'How were you going to handle those two by yourself?'

'I would have used the pistol in my purse. Next, I would have asked the man being swindled to lend a hand. We would have contacted the conductor for additional help in confining the two until we reached a town with a jail.'

He gave a nod of approval. 'I'm Brett Valeron,' he said. 'It's a pleasure to meet you, Miss . . . ?'

'Desiree Moore,' she reciprocated. 'I've been working for the Pinkerton agency for a little over six months.' Then with a curious lift to her groomed eyebrows, 'What about the prisoners? I

. . . I spent a lot of time trying to . . . '

'I'm on my way home.' He dismissed her concern. 'I'm sure you can manage their arrest and charges. However, I will lend you a hand in delivering them to the authorities.'

She did not hide her surprise . . . and delight. 'Really? You don't want any of the credit?'

'You were on their scent. If it hadn't been for that third man, I'm sure you would have gotten the other two without much effort.'

She displayed a grateful mien at once. 'That's very generous of you. I get bonus pay when I stop a scam or uncover a crooked porter or conductor.'

'My pay is the same whether I bring in the bad guys or not.'

'Valeron?' she repeated his surname. 'Any relation to the family that owns the cattle empire and township over on the Colorado-Wyoming border?'

'My father is Locke Valeron,' he acknowledged. 'He and his two brothers started the ranch together back when I was a teen. It grew considerably and now has a coal mine, lumber business and we operate several other stores or businesses in town.'

'Yet you chose to be a marshal?'

'I might settle on the ranch one day, but I always had a notion to get out and see some of the world. I wandered into a feud one day and ended up taking a hand. That earned me a couple of deputy U.S. Marshal chores and I was promoted and given a territory to look after.'

'I've heard of Valeron, but never been to the town itself. I spend most of my time on the train, either going to or coming from one place to another. The railroads like to keep their profits, rather than have them siphoned off by crooked employees. Plus, there are a lot of shifty characters trying to relieve the immigrants of what little money they have.'

'All that travel and work must cut down on the time you have for courtship.'

Desiree hid her emotions behind lowered lids, the first sign of insecurity she had shown. 'I'm not looking for a husband just yet. I want to experience some adventure in my life first.'

'I always thought marriage was about the biggest adventure a person could have.'

'I suppose, but I don't fancy having a man in my life right now.'

'Unless he has broken the law and you can arrest him,' he teased.

The remark brought a slender smile to her lips. 'Yes, that's it exactly.'

2

The telegram had arrived minutes before Wyatt led his cousins to the freight and express office in Valeron. Skip Andrews was behind the counter and greeted them with a solemn expression.

'It's powerful bad news about Scarlet and the death of her betrothed,' he began. 'The wire from Pueblo don't sound very promising, either.'

'Let's hear it,' Jared prompted. 'Do we have an idea of where to start our search?'

'Your pa wired that one man who might be involved was recognized . . . name of Waco. The place they are headed might be a bandit stronghold down in Arizona territory, a place called Brimstone. Locke says Mr Logan saw four men but there might have been more. The hostler at the livery sold a carriage and horse to a group of six men the morning of the attack — likely the same bunch.'

Jared looked at Wyatt. 'You ever hear of anyone named Waco?'

'The Waco Kid,' Wyatt replied. 'Been some time since he surfaced this far north-east, but he was a holy terror down around New Mexico and Texas a couple years back.'

'What about that odd sounding burg?' Shane asked. 'I never heard of Brimstone.'

'There was a rumor when I was working the Kettle-Masterson feud, over in Kansas a while back. One of the hired men who rode with us for a time said he'd heard about an outlaw refuge where the law never showed a badge. He said it had an odd name and was in Arizona, surrounded by a hundred miles of nothing. It was built and operated by a long-time bandit and some of his gunmen. I'll bet he was referring to Brimstone.'

'I'm sorry,' Skip said, 'but that's all

Locke and Temple learned. Sounds as if most of their information is guesswork.'

'We'll take the train to Utah and then head south,' Jared suggested. 'With a kidnapped woman, those men will be traveling off the main trails. We shouldn't be but a day or two behind them.'

Cliff's shoulders drooped. 'Dad-gum, it's 400 miles from Salt Lake City to the Arizona border. It'll take us a week to get there.'

'If they stick to a horse and buggy,' Wyatt opined, 'it will take the kidnappers nearly as long.'

'Any word from Brett?' Shane asked the telegrapher.

'I sent wires to every station along the line where he was last working,' Skip told the group. 'Hopefully, he will get one of them.'

'Be nice to have him along,' Wyatt said. 'If this turns out to be an entire town of outlaws, we'll need his expertise . . . and his gun.'

'Don't matter if he shows or not,'

Jared vowed. 'Them skunks are gonna die hard and fast, soon as we catch up with them. They grabbed Scarlet and killed her would-be husband. No way any of them will walk away from that. No way in hell!'

The telegraph sprang to life and Skip hurried to scribble the message. He told the men to stand by and frowned after he had signed off.

'This here is a follow-up from Locke,' he told the group. 'He wants me to send a runner out to the ranch. He has a chore for Reese.'

'Martin rode in with us to find out where we were headed and see if there was any other news. He can take the message for Reese.'

'What kind of chore is it?' Wyatt asked.

'It reads: *Reese, go to Cheyenne. See Nash. Pick up RJ and meet Jared at Brimstone.*'

'Who's RJ?' Cliff wanted to know.

'Must be someone Nash knows,' Jared said. 'Maybe it's a gent who has been to Brimstone.'

Shane said, 'Give the message to Martin and let's get going. We need to reach the train station before the next train going west. It'll save our horses for the first leg of the journey and we can get some shut-eye during the trip.'

Cliff snorted. 'You ever try and snooze on one of those bench seats? It's about the same as while riding in a stagecoach!'

'Let's pick up whatever supplies we need and get a move on.' Jared stuck to their task. 'We don't want to miss the next available train.'

★   ★   ★

Brett took charge of the three land swindlers and hired a youngster, who hustled tips helping folks with luggage, to tend to his horse and watch their belongings. Then he and Desiree escorted the trio of crooks to the sheriff's office. Soon as they were behind bars, they made their way to the telegraph office so she could report the arrest to the Pinkerton agency. The company would in turn contact the railroad and charges would be filed against the three men.

Brett was by the girl's side as they entered the express office, which also handled mail and the telegraph. He was somewhat surprised when the man running the place recognized him.

'Marshal Valeron!' he greeted with a smile. 'Been a coon's age.'

'I'm surprised you remember me. I only sent one message from here and that was a year ago.'

'I've got a *predilection* for faces,' he boasted. 'I have two wires for you. I was going to send one of the town runners over to the railroad station, in case you were aboard.'

Brett took the papers, read the scribbled words and frowned. 'When did these arrive?'

'The one about the kidnapping come in yesterday; the other was this morning.'

He had the telegrapher send a reply.

Next, he told Desiree what had happened, finishing with: 'My father and uncle seem to think it was a band of outlaws from a stronghold near the Arizona-Colorado border called Brimstone. One man was identified as the Waco Kid.'

'Brimstone?' Desiree repeated, aghast. 'It's reputed to be a town full of killers, robbers and thieves. Even the Army avoids that place.'

'How do you know so much about it?'

'I read all of the reports from our field agents. One of our Eyes tracked a couple of train robbers down there, but he was caught snooping. He got beat up, tied over his horse and told never to come back. He was lucky a prospector found him or he'd have died.'

'Sounds like the leaders of that stronghold protect their own.'

'We kept an open file on the two men, waiting until they surface again. It was deemed too dangerous to try and mount any kind of arrest.'

'Why take my sister?' he wondered.

'Pueblo, Colorado, is a long way from Arizona.'

'Perhaps for ransom?'

'They made no demand for payment,' he said. 'I need to make connections in Denver. The Atchison, Topeka and Santa Fe Railway is completed as far as Albuquerque. I can take the train as far as possible, then head for this Brimstone place once I cross into New Mexico.'

Desiree was suddenly aflutter. 'I've an idea!' she squealed like an excited child. 'I'll wire my office about our three prisoners and tell them I'm joining up with you.'

Brett gave her a sharp look of disapproval. 'What?'

'Yes,' she replied. Then talking quickly, 'Don't you see? I can check around Brimstone and see if our two train robbers are there. At the same time, I can be a big help to you in locating your sister.'

'And how do you intend to do that?'

'I have a decent voice and know a

number of songs by heart,' she said. 'I can enter town as an entertainer and offer to sing at one of their saloons.'

'You can't risk your neck like that. What if you're caught? You could end up a prisoner or even get yourself killed.'

She smiled enticingly. 'I'll be safe enough, if I have a personal bodyguard along.'

It was a ridiculous idea. Brett was ready to tell her the answer was *No, not a chance! Never!* And yet the idea had merit. The Pinkerton man had been caught and driven out of town. Brett could have entered pretending to be a criminal, but this way he would not be suspected.

'I don't know,' he voiced his concern. 'This place sounds like the most dangerous stronghold in the country. I'd never forgive myself if anything happened to you.'

'You helped me when I was in trouble,' Desiree pointed out. 'I'd like to return the favor.' She hurried to add,

'Plus, it will be a big step for the few women working for Pinkerton. It would show Al and the rest that we can handle risky undercover situations, too.'

'Brimstone probably isn't the best town to test a new job skill,' Brett replied. 'If we both end up dead, it would be a major setback for any other female agent for years to come.'

She ignored his pessimism. 'I need to stop in Denver and buy a fashionable dress for my audition. Otherwise, I've got everything I need.'

'Really, miss, I don't like the idea of . . . '

A stubborn expression clouded her otherwise comely features. 'I'm going with you or without you, Marshal. It would be a benefit if we entered town together. Safer for you, safer for me.'

Brett uttered a sigh. He knew Jared and some of the others would be pounding leather or riding the rails, rushing to the outlaw stronghold. It would be a big help if they could get someone working from the inside.

He sighed at Desiree's smug, yet pixie expression. 'If we can manage a way to catch the two men you're after, that's fine. But the first order of business is to rescue my sister, even if it means sneaking out in the dead of night to keep from facing off against fifty gunmen.'

She grinned. 'Either way, I'll have proven myself. That's the whole point of my going.'

'All right, Miss Moore,' he said at last. 'We'll stop at Denver long enough to buy you an outfit. Then we'll go to Brimstone and see what we can learn . . . while trying not to get ourselves killed.'

★   ★   ★

The headaches had finally subsided enough that Scarlet didn't accept another sip of laudanum from the man who seemed to be in charge of her care. Even so, the carriage ride was uncomfortable, bumpy and did little to ease the throb beneath her skull. Once alert, Scarlet studied covertly the six men who had taken her prisoner. It didn't take any prolonged study to realize escape was not an option. The gang avoided every town, one or more of the men was on constant guard, and the leader of the group seldom took his eyes off of her. After a time, she learned the names and traits of her kidnappers.

Dillon was sizable, perhaps six feet tall, although he was definitely not agile or physically fit like her brothers. The worst thing about him, other than the fact he hadn't shaved or bathed in weeks, was the lewd coveting in his constant yearning looks. His leering gaze left her feeling unclean.

As for the remainder, Waco dressed better than the others, shaved almost every day, and acted the most gentlemanly. Elmo, Sike and Ricky were vulgar and uncouth thugs. Landau seemed out of place with the band and took pains to see to her comfort. Other than being her primary guard, he paid her the least amount of attention. He brought her meals, water, and allowed her privacy when needed, but seldom spoke. Once, she overheard Elmo snicker about him being a nursemaid to the captive. His reply was, 'I've done things I'm not proud of, but I never intentionally harmed a woman or child,' which brought another snort of contempt from Elmo.

During the day, dust boiled up from the wheels and hooves of the horses to infiltrate the buggy's interior. Scarlet opted for comfort over privacy and tied the curtains back to allow in the fresh air. One of the men remarked they would be a week on the trail and it was like being hit in the stomach. How long would Dillon keep his distance? From the chatter, she had learned he intended to marry her. The news doubled the terror of being in the company of six ruthless kidnappers.

Closing her eyes, she softly prayed, 'Please, God, help my family to find me . . . but don't let any of them die on my behalf. Amen.'

★ ★ ★

Brett and Desiree rode in the family part of the immigrant car. They had suffered poor meals at the station stops and the wooden benches were not made for comfort. As evening approached, those who had two benches to share used the boards provided by the porters and turned the pair of benches to face each other. By laying the boards from bench to bench, it made a makeshift couch wide enough for two. Place a cushion at the head and lay with one's feet to the engine and it was possible to lie down. Thankfully, the car wasn't overcrowded, or they would have been forced to try and sleep sitting up.

As Brett helped Desiree get situated, he felt a nervous tingle. He hadn't slept next to a woman since he had rescued an Arapaho maid from a couple of Pawnee warriors. Then the arrangement had been necessary to ward off the twenty-degree weather and keep from freezing. He did recall how warm that girl had kept him that night and wondered if women were naturally more warm-blooded than men.

Battling to control his awkwardness, he hid his misgivings and stretched out on the bench next to the girl. It was a dark night and the rattle, bump and rumble of the wheels took some getting used to. He had almost managed to relax when Desiree whispered something he didn't quite make out.

'What?' he asked her.

She giggled. 'I said, this is the first time I ever slept with a man.'

'I believe,' he retorted, 'it would be more befitting to think of our arrangement as your sleeping *next to* a man.'

'Yes, I suppose so, but I never had any brothers. I was the eldest of four girls and spent most of my childhood raising my sisters.'

Brett laughed. 'I shared a bedroom with my brothers until I was about fifteen. We had three bedrooms in the house — one for the boys, another for the girls, and the folks had one to themselves. I always envied my sisters,

41

because there's only two of them — they each had their own bed and side of the room. We four boys shared two bunk beds.'

'I guess most people have heard of Valeron . . . a ranch and holdings that is measured in miles, not in acres. Even have a town with your name on it. That makes you kind of famous.'

Brett changed the subject. 'How did you end up working for Pinkerton?'

'By accident,' she replied. 'I took a trip from my home in Omaha to visit my aunt in Julesburg. Along the way, I noticed three men and a woman get on the train. They sat towards the front of the car and I was to the rear. When the man collecting tickets came around, something was passed to him that he put in his pocket. I was sure he had taken money and they were riding without tickets.

'I knew the conductor was an honest man so I told him about the four passengers. He came back personally to check tickets and the four people were put off at the next stop, along with the ticket taker. Rather than thank me, he wrote a deposition of the event and said I might inquire about a reward from the Pinkerton Agency.' She sighed. 'That was it. Next thing I knew, a man showed up to interview me, paid me a tidy sum for helping to rid the train of a profiteer, and provided me with a train pass and list of routes to take. I've turned in two different porters, a conductor and several swindlers or card sharps. The three men you helped me take down is the biggest operation I've been involved with.'

'And you really want to try this undercover operation in Brimstone?'

'I admit I'm a little nervous about it, but I want to help if I can. What is so different about a woman risking her life over that of a man?'

'Because a great number of men out West don't ever marry or have children,' Brett answered. 'A woman is important because she is needed to continue the population, to have and raise a family.'

'Don't you want a family some day?'

'More than anything.'

'Yet you risk your life on a daily basis to make it safer for everyone else. When do you get your turn to be a husband and father?'

'Well, it's unlikely to happen unless I meet the right woman.'

'Oh?' She immediately hid any sign of personal interest. 'And what kind of woman is that?'

Brett grinned. 'The usual things a man wants — thinks I walk on water, dotes on me endlessly, and lives only to make me happy.'

She uttered a sarcastic grunt. 'And what do you offer in return for a lady's fawning adulation?'

Turning serious, he looked at her. It was too dark to see her clearly, but he knew she was staring back. 'I'd give her anything in the world she wanted, if it was in my power. I'd make her a home, she'd share my future, and I would cherish her the rest of my life.'

Desiree actually said 'ahem' to clear her throat, then reciprocated. 'It sounds like a fair trade.'

'Just kiss her and let us get some sleep!' a guy muttered from a nearby bench.

'Uh, sorry,' Brett apologized. 'We're done talking.'

Desiree tittered softly and rotated her body to place her back to him. He wondered if the action insinuated she was avoiding any chance of an actual kiss, or possibly she was just getting comfortable. He knew one thing: he wouldn't get much sleep lying next to such a delectable woman!

★   ★   ★

The Valeron posse made it to a place called Nephi for the night. Seventy miles south of Salt Lake, it was a farming settlement, with mostly small cabins and several larger houses. The town store was like most in Utah, high-priced for travelers, but the people were friendly and called their local customers by name . . . adding a

Brother or *Sister* to their titles. One of them told Jared about a spot where there was fresh water and ample scrub brush for kindling. It was where they camped for the night.

Jared left his horse with Shane and set about preparing a fire pit for cooking their evening meal. Wyatt took a walk around the campsite for security's sake, even though the Indian wars in that area had ended several years back.

As the others laid out their beds for the night, Jared began frying up strips of ham in one pan and diced potatoes in a second. The coffee pot was beginning to perk as Wyatt dug out the tin plates and cups.

'Wonder if these Mormon gals go out for a little fun at nights?' Cliff asked no one in particular.

'You're worse than a tomcat,' Shane criticized him.

'Fourteen hours in the saddle isn't enough to tire you out for one day?'

Cliff chuckled. 'Shane, old buddy, you waste yourself only wooing one woman at a time, whilst there's a dozen standing around waiting in line. I do my best to give them all a little of my attention.'

'Like trying to put your grimy paws on Maria?'

Cliff grinned. 'I was doing it for you, cousin. If the gal said no to me, it would prove you were safe in courting her.'

'What a pal,' Wyatt sniggered, having listened to their exchange. 'Cliff was testing your girlfriend's fidelity. Not many men will sacrifice themselves for their kinfolk like that.'

Jared joined in. 'Yeah, look at the guy's dedication. Risking a beating from you, just so's you would know your gal is being faithful.'

Cliff glared over at Jared's back, as he was watching their meal. 'If you two yahoos hadn't butted in, I'd have found out if Maria truly does care about Shane.'

'If you'd have kissed her,' Shane warned, 'I'd have dropped the bucket along with the water on top of your head!'

Cliff displayed his usual cocky grin, while his tone was sarcastic. 'I didn't thank you for inviting Veta to the party. Now I'll have to work like the devil to get her back.'

'Well,' Wyatt interjected, 'you can always take another of those girls that's waiting in line. You said there were a bunch of them.'

'It's going to be a long ride, if I'm the only one you boys have to badger.'

'Don't blame us,' Jared said. 'Every time you open your mouth, you give us new ammunition.'

'You think Scarlet is at Brimstone by now?' Shane changed the conversation.

'Not yet,' Wyatt guessed. 'I figure the kidnappers will beat us by a day or two.'

'What about Reese? You think him and RJ will get there ahead of us?'

'Don't see how. Even if they take the train down to New Mexico, they will have a long ride back north to reach Brimstone. We should be there before them.'

'Those outlaws will be watching for

anyone new coming to town,' Jared warned.

'Brett probably knows about the kidnapping by now. He might reach Brimstone before us.'

'I hope you're right, Shane,' Jared said. 'Be nice to have him with us before we enter town. He ought to have an idea or two about how we can tackle so many outlaws at one time.'

'You think there will be all that many?' Cliff asked.

'It's unlikely every man in town would fight to stop us from taking Scarlet back,' Wyatt replied. 'But it is a town full of gunmen, killers and thieves. They might have a code in place about protecting every man within the confines of the stronghold.'

'That's a cheery thought,' Cliff said.

'Odds don't matter,' Jared commented. 'We don't leave until Scarlet is free and the kidnappers are dead. If that means a fight, then a fight is what they'll get.'

'A half dozen of us?' Cliff worried.

'Against a hundred guns?'

'You volunteered for this,' Wyatt told him. 'You want out, you can head for home tomorrow.'

'Not me!' he stated emphatically. Then with a twisted smirk, 'Might be a woman or two around. Could be you will need me to either interrogate or sweep one off her feet. None of you clods have the finesse to handle a delicate job like that.'

'Or we might need someone to hold and clean up after the horses,' Shane quipped. 'I think that's equally in line with your qualifications.'

'Personally,' Wyatt joked, 'I like the idea of taking Cliff along. If we need a quick getaway, we can leave him behind to slow down the pursuit. Won't be anyone who misses him back at the ranch.'

'Thanks, buddy,' he drawled. 'It's nice to know you care.'

'Grub is ready,' Jared prevented any more levity. 'Bring over your plates.'

3

The gang needed fresh mounts, so Waco and Dillon left the group with horses in tow to make the swap at a small settlement. Meanwhile, the others took advantage of the free time to prepare a cooked meal and get an extra hour's rest.

Landau brought a tin plate with chilli and a chunk of bread to Scarlet. Then he stayed close so no one got any notions of visiting the girl.

'You are not like the others,' Scarlet commented, after eating a small portion of the food.

Landau glanced at her. 'No?'

Scarlet took advantage of their privacy. 'I think you made a mistake of some kind, probably in the heat of the moment. I see no malice or savagery in your make-up.'

'You are such a good judge of

character, are you?'

'I've four brothers, a sister and a host of cousins. I have been around men all my life. I've seen the good, the bad, the caring and the selfish. Even though you are with these kidnappers and murderers, you seem to have a genuine concern for my welfare.'

'Don't mistake my protective nature as a weakness,' he warned. 'My first loyalty is to the men I'm riding with.'

Scarlet smiled at his declaration. 'I'm sorry but I don't believe you.'

The confusion that swept his features belied his steadfast resolve. She discerned the man had honor, regardless of his recent actions. In an effort to win an ally, she asked, 'What did you do to wind up sharing your life with these outlaws?'

'It's not something I care to talk about.'

'I'm your prisoner,' she stated the obvious. 'Your friends killed my would-be husband and kidnapped me. You can't be afraid I will judge you harshly. What could you have possibly done that is worse than this?'

Landau's defiant expression melted away and he lowered his head, guilt-ridden. 'I killed my wife and her lover,' he admitted, his words barely audible.

Scarlet felt her mouth fall open. As she attempted to appreciate the gravity of his statement, he exhaled a breath of air and continued.

'The gal I married had worked in a saloon. I was only one of her many . . . *suitors*,' he used a sympathetic term for her profession. 'She claimed she had been forced into a life of servitude, abandoned by a family that could no longer support all of their children. She wanted to get away from the degrada-tion of her occupation and start a new life. I believed her.'

Landau stared blindly off into the distance and went on with his tale. 'I had nothing, but I took a job at a nearby ranch. The work was hard and I often didn't get home until late.' His face darkened at a terrible memory.

'But my wife got tired of the hard work, being broke, and became bored with having only one man in her life. I returned without warning one day . . .'

Landau grit his teeth.

'I saw the horse tied out in front of the house. When I threw open the door, the two of them were together — the town Romeo and my wife!' His voice had grown ice cold. 'The guy reached for the gun he had draped over the bedpost and I shot him twice in the chest.'

Scarlet moistened her lips with her tongue and whispered, 'It was a moment of rage for a terrible betrayal. Any man might have reacted the same way.'

Landau shook off the reverie and returned to the present. He looked at Scarlet as if surprised to discover she had overheard his confession. With a genuine sorrow, he added a fatal note, 'The bullets went through the adulterer and one of them struck my wife in the head.'

'You didn't mean to kill her,' Scarlet said gently. 'It was an accident.'

Landau shook his head. 'Yes. I could never have killed her, not even after what she'd done. I loved that girl with my whole heart.'

'You know that most juries would have found you within your rights,' Scarlet told him. 'A man, when faced by such a degree of treachery, cannot be held accountable for his actions. Plus, you didn't intend to hurt your wife. Her death was not intentional.'

The man rebounded. 'What a grand lady you are,' he praised. 'Here you are, captive to a bunch of killers, your betrothed murdered, and you show sympathy for one of the men responsible.'

Scarlet lifted her chin. 'I am twenty-four years old and consider myself a good judge of character, Mr Landau. Besides, I didn't see you enter the house during the attack.'

'No, I handle the horses so I don't hurt or rob anyone. Poor excuse for a criminal.'

'Will Dillon ... ' She swallowed hard. 'Will he try to take me by force?'

'Not until we get home,' Landau said, squirming at the notion. 'He is taking you to meet his brother. Tynan is the boss over at Brimstone. He will ultimately decide your fate.'

'My fate is not in his hands — nor your own,' she vowed. 'My family will come for me. If you stand by these men, you will be killed.'

The man gave an off-hand gesture, as it if didn't matter. 'Dying is likely the only relief I'll ever get from the pain of losing my wife.'

'That's no excuse for riding with these men. However,' she softened her features, 'I'm glad you are here. I shouldn't want to face this journey, or Dillon, without you to look after my welfare.'

Landau didn't reply. He took her plate and returned to the company of the other men.

A few minutes later, Dillon arrived with fresh animals. They were quickly on the move and continued until the moon was high. It was midnight before they stopped to a cold camp. Six hours later, they were saddling up at daylight.

'She do any talking yet?' Dillon asked Landau, as the sun began to brighten the world.

'Only when she needs some privacy.' He was nonchalant. 'She doesn't drink but a few sips of water and eats very little of the food we're giving her.'

'At least she isn't trying to starve herself to death.'

'We made a big mistake grabbing her. You should have brought a girl somewhere along the line. This gal has been raised proper, and I suspect her kin might be formidable.'

'Why is that?' Dillon asked.

'She claims to come from a big family and warned they would be coming after us,' he related. 'And did you take a look at what she's wearing? Them shoes are from back east, and her wedding dress is expensive. Plus, she holds herself erect and proud, like nothing can dampen her spirit.'

'I'll enjoy breaking the little mustang. She'll bend to my will quick enough.'

'That's what I'm saying, Dillon. This ain't no mustang you tossed your loop at, she's a purebred, a genteel lady who might prefer death over surrender.'

'Since when did you become a judge of horseflesh or women?'

'I was married for a time.'

'Didn't work out, huh?' Dillon said with a grin. 'And now you are living on the run and pulling hold-ups with a gang of murderers.'

'I've shot a couple of people, too. I reckon I'll end up in Hell with the rest of you.'

Dillon turned to the present. 'Way I figure it, we should make Brimstone about sunset tomorrow. Tell the boys we're eating in the saddle. Tonight, we'll camp at dusk and rest the horses.'

'Before we pull out, I'll get an air-tight of beans and some hardtack for myself and the girl. We won't need to stop unless it's to rest the horses.'

'Tynan is going to be impressed by the haul we made.'

Landau remained serious. 'I hope he agrees with your choice for a wife. We've got a town full of gunmen, but we can't take on the Army, not if they decide to come after us in force.'

'You saw the size of that house in Pueblo. Those people didn't have money or social position.'

'They were a retired couple. Their son probably came home for the wedding. No telling what his job or position was. Besides, it's the girl's family we have to worry about.'

'Stop worrying,' Dillon said. 'Tynan is going to be blown away when he gets a look at that gal. Lucia is the queen of Brimstone — my girl is going to be the princess!'

'Yeah, right. All hail the new Princess of Brimstone,' he retorted. 'I just hope she doesn't turn out to be the Princess of Doom!'

★　★　★

Brett was stiff from trying to sleep on the wooden bench. He watched daylight come and a few people began to move about. During the night, Desiree had turned over restlessly. He happened to be looking at Desiree when her eyes blinked, then fluttered open. The green irises were visible in the dim light and he was awestruck at the young lady's contented expression. It caused him to wonder if she had been having a pleasant dream.

'Good morning,' he greeted her.

She winced at the effort to sit up, then paused to stretch her arms over her head. 'I've slept on much softer beds,' she complained.

'Constantly riding the train, you ought to be used to the less than luxurious accommodations.'

'How does one become accustomed to a physical beating for eight hours at a time?'

Brett took the blankets and was ready to remove the sleeping boards by the time Desiree was on her feet. He placed the two boards in the aisle for the porters and turned the one bench around so it faced in the right direction. As they sat down together, he asked, 'Have you traveled this far south before?'

'No. I've mostly stayed in Kansas, Nebraska or Colorado.'

'We should reach our station in an hour or two. One of the porters mentioned it is a regular stop, so the town has several stores and is of some size.'

'So we're not going all the way to Albuquerque?'

'No. This stop is the closest to our goal. We will ask around for directions to Brimstone. I'd estimate it's seventy to a hundred miles yet. We might make it there by late tomorrow.'

They arrived at their station a short time later. Brett had already spoken to the porter about offloading his horse and gear. Desiree collected their luggage at the same time. He joined the lady at the boarding platform and again hired a youth to watch their gear and his horse. Then the two of them walked through the small burg and found a blacksmith and stable at the far end of town. The owner had a single carriage suitable for a lady, although it had seen better days. The chaise, as the man called it, was lightweight and needed only one horse. The folding hood was frayed and faded from the weather, but it would be adequate to keep the sun off them during travel. Brett dickered with the man on a price for a horse, and they were ready to travel by the time the first train whistle blew.

After a quick meal, they bought a handful of supplies, including two kegs for water and a couple of blankets for Desiree's bedroll. Picking up their luggage and Brett's saddle, they stowed their belongings inside the carriage and put his horse on a lead rope at the back of the buggy. Within minutes, they had put the town behind them.

'The blacksmith said Brimstone was almost to the Colorado border . . . about eighty miles.'

Desiree sighed. 'Then we won't

arrive until tomorrow sometime.'

'Yep,' he agreed. Then looking downward, 'The cushion is worn out on this seat. You might want to fold one of your blankets to sit on. Going to be rough going between here and Brimstone.'

'I'm fine,' she said. 'Having any cushion at all is an improvement over the train. I did get back east on one assignment and got to try out one of the sleeping cars. It is a vast improvement over the Zulu cars used for transporting immigrants.'

'After two days of riding through this country in a carriage, you'll probably be yearning for a railroad car . . . any railroad car.'

'I'm sure I'll be feeling the effects of being bounced and jarred until my teeth rattle, long before we reach the bandit town.'

Brett checked the position of the sun and took a bearing on some distant mountains. 'We should hit a freight trail in an hour or so. Last chance to change your mind about singing.'

'I'll be all right,' Desiree assured him. 'I've sang in public a few times. I'm not shy when it comes to being in front of a crowd.'

'This will be performing for a bunch of drunkards, criminals and riffraff, some of the worst men in the territory. They might not be satisfied to simply listen.'

'I'll make it understood I only entertain with my voice and don't socialize with the customers.'

'It is still a risky undertaking,' he cautioned. 'I can stick by you for the most part, but I'll have to slip out of town every so often to keep watch for my family. We'll need to coordinate whatever plan we come up with.'

'My welfare is not your responsibility. I'm on an undercover operation. If I can do this, Mr Pinkerton might allow other women operatives to undergo the same type of activity.'

'Speaking for myself, I don't like the idea of a young lady getting into a situation where she might end up as a prisoner or slave . . . or worse.'

'That's why I have you as my bodyguard,' she said, displaying a smile.

'We'd best have a story in mind, in case I'm recognized.' He regarded her with a narrow look. 'If need be, can you shoot?'

'I have a gun in my handbag, a Remington Double Derringer.'

'Seen them a few times — fires two .41 Rimfire cartridges. Got any spare ammo?'

'Six bullets.'

He grunted. 'All the more reason to get our stories straight. If it comes to a fight, I don't think we can count on you for any real firepower.'

★　★　★

Scarlet ached from the constant confinement of the dusty carriage and felt downright grungy from not having a bath or changing clothes in nearly a week. When the gang finally reached their destination, Dillon was there to collect her.

She didn't balk at his taking her arm with one of his rough hands and pulling her out of the carriage. He gave her a moment to get her balance before he led her from the livery stable. She offered no resistance as she glanced around.

The town was made up of several wooden buildings and dozens of tents or wagons. Everything had been arranged to either side of the main street, with a sleazy looking saloon smack in the middle. Dust was an inch thick from wagons churning up the dirt, and horse leavings had been shoved into piles rather than being removed. The air reeked of manure, garbage and whiskey. A neatly painted sign above the double-door entrance of the two-storey saloon read: *The Snake Pit*. She took notice of a trading post and an eating place called Cookie's Hash House, a couple of other stores and a second smaller saloon. The disorder and trash, combined with a couple bunkhouse-like buildings, resembled a mining community, not an actual civilized population.

As it was past dark, the Snake Pit was

lit up more than any other place. A piano was playing and there was the raucous noise of rowdy men and the occasional shrill laugh of a woman. A few men were visible in and around their shelters, with lamps or fire-pits burning. Some were cooking meals, while others were sitting or standing around. From what little she could make out, it appeared nearly all the men were unshaven, with long hair and dirty clothes. Scarlet had to wonder if there was a bath house or barber within the confines of the outlaw settlement.

She stiffened as they approached the saloon but Dillon tightened his grip and kept walking. They passed through the bat-wing doors and the piano music stopped. All eyes turned on the new arrivals. It was unlikely a woman dressed in a wedding gown had ever set foot in this den of killers and thieves.

No fewer than forty men were inside the room. Some were at gambling tables, others playing cards, with a few standing about or at the main bar.

There were also several women, wearing garish clothes and thick paint on their faces. Most of them appeared to be past childbearing age, and not one appeared to have seen the wet side of a washcloth in weeks.

From within the acrid smoke and mix of beer and whiskey stench, a man in a tidy suit and string tie came striding across the crowded floor. He greeted the man at her side, while staring at her in puzzlement. 'Dillon, what on earth have you brought back with you?'

'Check her over good, big brother,' Dillon chortled. 'There ain't a finer woman to be found within 500 miles.'

The man eyed Scarlet from tip to top, but there was no warmth in his gaze. 'Where did you get the dress? And who did you buy her from . . . Indians? Comancheros?'

'Didn't cost me a cent,' Dillon boasted. 'We snatched her before her wedding.'

Tynan scowled at the news. 'Let's go

upstairs,' he ordered. 'Bring the girl and your loot.'

Dillon took the saddle-bags from Waco, who had followed along after him and Scarlet. He didn't offer to come along, nor did any of the others who had been traveling with them.

The stairway was located at the back of the saloon. Upstairs, the first room was obviously used as an office. Other doors along the hallway denoted more rooms. Scarlet counted eight altogether.

Tynan opened the first door and entered his office. A woman was seated behind the desk, working on a ledger of some kind. She lifted her eyes from her activity and gaped at seeing a lady in a wedding dress. However, she stood up, looked at Tynan and asked, 'Do you wish for me to leave?'

He gave a curt nod and she hurried from the room. When the door closed, he took possession of the saddlebags and dumped the contents on the desktop. He sorted through the cash, gold and coins.

'Good haul,' he praised his brother's

work. 'Ought to keep you and the boys for a spell.'

Dillon touted smugly, 'We'll pay our tabs and be set for months.'

Tynan rotated around and leaned against the desk. His arms were folded and he again gave Scarlet a long, hard stare. 'Who is the girl?'

'I spotted her over in Pueblo, Colorado, and decided she was the one I wanted.'

'Decked out for a wedding? That's how she was dressed when you grabbed her?'

'Weren't hard, Ty,' Dillon explained. 'Only one guy and a couple old people there. We tossed her in a wagon and lit out before anyone knew what happened. We left no trace.'

Tynan stepped forward until his breath was right in Scarlet's face. 'Who are you?'

Summoning her bravado, she answered, 'My name is Scarlet.'

He glanced over her clothes. 'High-priced dress and fancy shoes,' he began.

'Not a bit of tan from the sun and your hands look to have never done any hard physical work. Your pa own a business of some kind?'

'My father is a rancher in Colorado.'

'What's your last name?'

'It would have been Logan, if your brother hadn't killed the man I was about to marry.'

Tynan glowered at Dillon. 'You stole a bride *and* killed the groom!' His words were savagely critical. 'Are you out of your mind? What have I told you about killing? We never kill anyone unless it's absolutely necessary.'

'You said to get a girl on the trip,' Dillon countered. 'I wanted someone who was as much a lady as Lucia. You know, so they could socialize and such together.'

'What about a posse? Kidnapping a bride and killing her soon-to-be husband? You'll have a hundred men on your trail.'

Dillon snickered at the idea. 'Not a soul seen us leave town. We kept watch

71

the first day or two, but there was never anyone on our back trail. It's like I told you, we got away clean.'

Tynan knew what was done could not be undone. He said, 'She looks a little young for you.'

'Hey, you said we ought to have some kids, a real family. I wanted one young enough to give me three or four.' He added, 'You're the one who said we were going to make this place into a regular town. Way things been going, I didn't figure it would be long before that happened.'

'You're right about that, Dillon, but I didn't intend for you to steal a bride. You were supposed to buy a wife like I did with Lucia.'

'Yeah, but you thought you were getting a wife who could have kids. Lucia was barren and you're almost forty. I didn't want to take a chance on being sold a bum horse.'

'Put her in the spare room for now. We'll talk about this later.'

Dillon took Scarlet down to the room

at the very end of the hall. It had a latch on the outside so it could be used to lock someone inside.

'Don't worry,' he said in a suggestive tone of voice, 'soon as you've accepted your situation, I'll treat you like a royal princess.'

Scarlet did not reply, but walked into the sparsely furnished room and stood with her hands clasped in front of her.

'Good night, sweetheart,' Dillon gushed. 'Sweet dreams . . . of me and you together!'

Silent still, she remained motionless while he closed and locked the door.

Having taken a quick survey of the room, she knew it had a cot, a nightstand and a couple of hooks on the wall to hang clothing. There was no lamp or candle and no window. Left standing in the complete blackness, Scarlet felt her way to the bed. She used a hand and swept it over the blanket, making sure it was clear of insects or debris. With nothing else to do, she sat down on the bunk. Resting her elbows on her knees, she placed her head between her hands and allowed herself a few tears. She had been forced to be strong throughout the kidnapping and transport, day after day, never able to relax or let down her guard. It had taken its toll.

Her dark sanctuary was short-lived. Someone began fiddling with the door latch!

Scarlet quickly dabbed at the tears to remove any moisture. She still had the backs of her knuckles on her cheeks when the door opened and a lamp shone brightly inside the room. She shielded her eyes against the glare and saw it was the woman — Lucia, she supposed — the one who had been sitting at Tynan's desk.

'I'm told you haven't had anything to eat since this morning, you poor dear,' she said, sympathy thick in her voice.

Scarlet didn't reply as the woman entered and hooked the lamp over one of the wall hooks. She also had a pitcher of water and a glass, which she placed on the nightstand. 'I have the cook warming a plate of stew.' She lifted a shoulder in a shrug. 'It is all he had to offer this time of night.'

'Thank you.'

Lucia stood and looked at Scarlet for a time. 'That's a beautiful dress you're wearing, even after so much travel. I will bring you something else to wear, so the gown might be preserved.' When Scarlet did not respond, she tried another approach. 'I heard someone say you came from Colorado.'

'It's where my affianced was killed and I was kidnapped.'

'Tynan is very angry about this. He has always been against killing or the abduction of women or children.'

'That is of little comfort, considering my predicament.'

'You don't talk like a farm girl.'

It was a statement, so Scarlet replied, 'My family owns a ranch and all of the children are educated by my mother and two aunts.'

'I'm sorry this has happened to you.

Dillon is always trying to please Tynan. I believe he chose you because you are a lady.' She displayed a mirthless smile. 'He thinks I'm also a lady.'

'The man's a murderer and kidnapper. If he touches me, he will be a molester, too.'

'I'm sorry,' Lucia repeated her apology. 'There's nothing I can do.'

'I will never agree to a forced marriage with that vile beast,' Scarlet said firmly. 'I don't care what threat you hold over my head.'

Lucia sighed, displaying worry and empathy. 'It doesn't matter what you want, dear. You won't be given a choice. The one who will perform the marriage here is Parson. I don't even know his real name, but he was once a preacher, before he killed a man in a fight over a woman.'

'So any form of wedding will be a sham. I won't be given a chance to refuse to take Dillon as my husband?'

'No,' Lucia continued, 'The ceremony will be about two minutes and then it will be drinks and food all around until everyone is drunk.'

'I've never had to test my bravery before, but I come from a strong and honorable family. If I am forced into a mendacious wedlock, I will find a way to escape. If that is impossible, I will kill my abusive captor in his sleep.'

Lucia was shocked by the solemn oath. 'Senorita! You cannot mean that.'

'I do mean it. My family is renowned for their strength and tenacity. If my father, uncles, brothers and cousins don't arrive in time to save me from a forced marriage, I will fight to protect my honor. I will never submit to a kidnapper and murderer. I will die first — comforted by the knowledge that everyone who had anything to do with my being here will also die!'

Tynan's wife reeled from witnessing such resolute vows. 'Who are your family?' she queried. 'From where do you draw such courage?'

'My name is Scarlet Valeron.'

Lucia backed up, as if the surname

had been a slap to her face. She did not speak again, but scampered out the door and closed it behind her. Then her steps were hurried as she went down the hallway.

4

Shane was tending to the string of tethered horses while his three cousins finished clearing the camp and packing their gear. Cliff wandered over to the horses and saw Shane had chosen one of the spare mounts to ride. It was a peculiar looking white mare with a number of black spots scattered from rump to her ears, plus a mottled mane and a skunk-colored tail. Even her legs were unevenly color-matched, with two blackish stockings and two a dirty white.

'What the Sam Hill did you bring that mongrel looking jackass for?' Cliff snorted. 'She's gotta be the most ugly horse I ever saw!'

Shane caught Wyatt and Jared's eye before answering. They moved casually over to their own mounts, but kept a close watch on what transpired between the two.

'Easy there, Beauty,' Shane spoke to the mare, stroking her neck and speaking into her ear. 'Bad old cousin Cliff don't know what he's talking about.'

Cliff roared with laughter. '*Beauty!* You named her Beauty!' Another chortle. 'What on earth is beautiful about that nag?'

'Ignore that mean-mouthed moron,' Shane told the horse in a conciliatory tone of voice.

Cliff sniggered his disdain as he placed his horse blanket on the back of his steed. As he turned to grab his saddle, Shane tapped the side of Beauty's neck.

Quick as the strike of a snake, Beauty used her teeth to grab the blanket from the other horse and tossed her head, flinging the blanket ten feet away. Then, just as quickly, she lowered her head, as if seeking some grass.

Cliff hefted the saddle and hooked one stirrup over the horn, before he saw the blanket was missing. He stopped in mid-motion and looked around.

Shane was on the opposite side of

Beauty, so he could not have moved the blanket, and Beauty was nibbling at a weathered sagebrush.

'What the hell?' Cliff grumbled under his breath. Then he put the saddle down, retrieved the blanket and again smoothed it over the back of his mount. Soon as he rotated about to reach for the saddle, Shane tapped Beauty again. She whipped her head around, once more taking the blanket between her teeth and giving it a toss.

Cliff picked up the saddle, ready once more, and again saw the blanket was missing. He dropped the rig and put his hands on his hips, staring at Shane.

'All right, wise acre! How are you doing that from over there?'

'Doing what?' Shane asked in total innocence.

'Come on, Cliff!' Jared snapped sharply. 'Do you need help to saddle your own horse?'

This time, Cliff led his horse a short distance from Shane and Beauty, before recovering the blanket. He was the last to get mounted, still muttering about the magical, disappearing blanket.

As they started down the trail, Jared rode alongside of Shane. 'That the horse you bought from the traveling circus last summer?'

'Smart as can be, this horse,' he bragged. 'She can do a number of tricks.' With a grin, 'And she is the fastest horse at swiping a blanket I ever saw.'

'It wouldn't work if she hadn't been trained to immediately start nibbling grass or the like.'

'I thought she might come in handy,' Shane said. 'She is good for a diversion, because she will go just about any place . . . even into a saloon or store. The owner claimed she slept in his hotel room one time, and he was on the second floor!'

'It's a wonder he parted with her.'

'He was retiring and going to live with his kids. They had a small house in a city, with no yard. They drew the line at him keeping the horse inside like a pet.' Jared didn't offer anything further, so Shane glanced back at his two cousins. 'I noticed Wyatt leave camp for a short while last night. He seems to disappear quite often.'

'Practising,' Jared informed Shane. 'Man gets a rep with a gun, he never knows when he might have to use it. You notice his cut-away holster is never dusty or dry. He uses neatsfoot oil to keep the leather soft and malleable. A stiff holster can cost you a split second if you have to get your gun out quick.'

'Has Wyatt killed many men?'

'A few, but they were all trying to kill him right back. Being a troubleshooter for ranches, mines and even a few towns, he's been in some difficult situations. Tell you one thing, cuz, I'm glad he's riding with us on this trip.'

'Think we'll get there by tomorrow night?'

'Probably the day after. We've made pretty good time, but fifty miles a day is about all we can average with the number of hills we've had to climb.'

Shane groaned. 'You know Scarlet and me grew up together, being born the same year. I hate to think of her being the prisoner of a bunch of robbers, murderers and thieves.'

'You're in no more hurry than me,' Jared avowed, his jaw clenched in hate. 'When I think of her being taken against her will, about what they intend to do with her . . . ' He didn't have to finish.

'It's more than I can stand, Jer.'

'We can only go as fast as we can. You know the horses; dare we run them every other mile? That would add some distance for us.'

'We might need their stamina to escape from Brimstone. I don't want to risk tiring them out too much. They are getting by without much water as it is.'

'A creek is on the map, one we should make later today. We'll stop for an hour or two so the horses can drink their fill and graze whatever grass we find along the riverbanks.'

'It's the smart play,' Shane concurred.

'We still have to worry about what to do once we reach Brimstone. Wyatt said he could ride in as a wanted man and maybe take one of us with him, but four of us showing up?' Jared gave his head a shake. 'That would raise suspicion in a hurry.'

'We ought to wait for Reese. The fellow he was supposed to meet at Cheyenne might offer us a way in.'

'Be nice to have Brett show up, too. We get six or seven of us, we'll have a lot more options.'

'There's one thing certain,' Shane avowed. 'Anyone and everyone involved with Scarlet's kidnapping is going to pay for it!'

'That's the truth, cuz. It sure is.'

★　★　★

Dillon sat, his temper barely contained, with shoulders bowed, listening to the verbal lashing. Tynan was fuming, pacing the office and wringing his hands like a worried husband on the eve of his first child's delivery.

'Of all the stupid, idiotic things to do,' he continued to rant. 'You pick on the most powerful family in the country — steal one of their women and kill her would-be husband. Dammit all, Dillon! You might as well have grabbed the governor's daughter!'

'I didn't know she was anyone special!' Dillon fired back. 'She was marrying some bum whose folks lived in a dinky little house in the middle of town. How could I have known the gal was a Valeron?'

'You should have found out! Why the blazes didn't you do like I told you and buy a wife? For a couple hundred dollars, you could have had your pick of farmers, immigrants, Indians or señoritas!'

'I wanted someone special,' Dillon maintained. 'Soon as I laid eyes on this gal, I knew she was the one for me.'

'You ever hear of Wyatt Valeron?' Tynan growled. 'He put down the miner's strike at Gold Ridge. He took Silas Crow and his brother in a shootout outside of

Meeker. They had been robbing stages and terrorizing the country until Valeron tracked them down.'

'Yeah, I know . . . a regular hell-on-the-hoof gunman.'

'Another Valeron is a U.S. Marshal!' Tynan wailed. 'You couldn't have picked a worse family to kidnap a girl from if you searched from here to Saint Louis!'

'Can't worry about it now,' Dillon muttered. 'I took her and I'm keeping her.'

Tynan threw his arms in the air with his frustration. 'You're putting us all at risk. That family won't let this go. They'll come after us and won't quit until we're dead!'

'We got a hundred men here at any one time,' Dillon argued. 'Ain't no family big enough to do battle with us.'

'You're not thinking with your head. The outlaws in Brimstone are here because the law doesn't bother us. They aren't going to defend us against a small army, not for stealing an innocent girl on her wedding day. If it comes to a major battle, most of the men here will ride away and let us stand alone. We've got no more than a dozen men we can count on if this comes to a fight.'

'They ain't never gonna find her down here, Ty. This is the badlands, with us being the only town in a hundred miles in any direction. We don't have nothin' to worry about.'

'Didn't you hear what I said? That family won't stop . . . not ever!'

Dillon anchored his teeth. 'I ain't giving her up! She's mine!'

To argue was a waste of time and breath. Tynan knew his brother could be stubborn. It was a family trait. Still, he had a very bad feeling about this. Lucia had been near hysteria when she came to him with the news. And she was pretty much guiltless. She had been sold to him like a horse, but she was a survivor and a realist. She made the best of her situation and they had made a good life together. It frightened her that Dillon had pulled such a dumb stunt. It was a threat to them all, to their future.

'You better use some of that loot you accumulated to hire sentries to guard the outskirts of town. If anyone comes snooping, we need to know about it — pronto!'

'Sure, Ty,' Dillon agreed. 'I'll handle it.'

'About your wedding,' he ordered. 'You'll need to delay that a few days, until we make certain no one has followed you here.'

Dillon looked like he might object, but Tynan gave him a hard look and added, 'It will also give your bride a chance to get used to the idea. It would be better if she wasn't kicking and screaming throughout the whole ceremony. Once she knows her fate is cast, she might accept her situation.'

'How long do I gotta wait?'

'A coupla weeks ought to be enough. If no one has shown up by then we ought to be safe.'

'One week,' Dillon countered. 'I ain't gonna wait no more'n a week.'

Tynan knew this was the best

arrangement he would get without a fight. 'All right. Lucia will take meals and see to her needs. I'll have her try and convince the girl that there are no options to the marriage. You keep your distance for now. After we've tried to reason with her for a few days, you can try talking to her. But if you touch a hair on her head before the vows, I won't try and stop her from figuring out a way to kill you.'

'I ain't scar't a' no woman.'

'Listen to me, Dillon!' he snarled. 'You dishonor a lady of her caliber and you won't be welcome in this town . . . not by anyone!'

'Geez, big brother, anyone would think we was raised by a church-going family.'

'You chose her because she was a proper lady,' Tynan reminded him. 'You can't treat her like a tramp or some vagabond you bought off the street. You have to at least pretend to respect her.'

'OK, big brother. I'll let her be until we are hitched. Satisfied?'

Tynan gave a bob of his head. 'Get those guards posted. Now. Tonight!'

'Yeah, yeah,' Dillon grumbled. 'Be too damn bad if the bogeyman sneaked into town.'

'A bogeyman is for frightening children,' Tynan countered. 'I'm concerned about the *Pale Horseman*, the bringer of death.'

'You quoting the Parson now? He used them very words that time we kilt that priest.'

'*You* killed the priest,' Tynan corrected. 'I told you to let him alone.'

'He kept shouting and threatening us for shooting them two trappers and taking their horses and pelts.' With a snort, 'As if them two hunters ever attended his church meetings!'

Tynan sighed at his brother's ignorance. 'He was threatening our souls, not physical violence.'

'Well, I don't take that from nobody,' Dillon declared. 'He got what he asked for.'

'Get going.' Tynan didn't debate

further. 'Let me know when the guards are in place.'

* * *

'This looks like a good spot to camp,' Brett remarked, turning the buggy into a clearing between a tangle of oak brush and pinyon. The chaparral formed a semi-circle to cut off the evening wind and there was a patch of wild grass here and there for the horses.

Desiree looked skyward. 'No clouds in sight. I suppose we can make do.'

'You can sleep here in the carriage. Be a little cramped, but you can probably manage to curl up on the seat cushion.'

'No, thanks,' she replied. 'Give me enough room where I can stretch out. Last night in the train car was worse than sleeping on the ground.'

'I thought it was pretty cosy myself.'

'Is that why you were walking hunched over this morning?' she teased. 'Isn't cosy a word that means the same as comfortable?'

Brett grinned. 'I reckon I was referring more to the company. My horse would have been green with jealousy, seeing us snuggled up together the way we were.'

'I don't recall any snuggling,' she riposted puritanically. 'And there were twenty-six other passengers and a porter or two wandering around during the night. If you're used to that many people, you must really come from a big family.' She shook her head. 'How big did you say your ranch is?'

'We've three main houses, one each for my father and two uncles. I told you that my family has four boys and two girls. Well, Temple has two boys and three girls. As for Udall, he has three boys and a girl. There's also a cousin or two around most of the time, too. The houses share a corral, tool shed and a barn big enough for the passenger car we have. Milk cows, pigs, goats, chickens, and several hundred acres under plow for corn, beans, potatoes and the like. We grow our own wheat and cut wild grass for hay.

'There's several thousand head of cattle, a coal mine, lumberyard and grinding mill on the ranch and a half dozen stores in town belong to our family. I'd guess we have more than a hundred full-time employees and twice that during the summer months.'

Desiree had to remind herself to close her mouth. 'I knew it was large, but your family's property is practically a small country.'

'My father and uncles wanted to be independent in their needs.'

'So why become a marshal? There is surely enough work for you on your family's ranch.'

'I wanted to do something with my life,' he answered. 'My brother, Nash, went off to college and became a doctor. Cousin Wyatt took on a town-taming job and makes a living with his gun. Scarlet was about to become the wife of a man who worked in the logging industry. She would have moved to Oregon with him. Yet, we have our own lumber business, had the man chosen to work with our family. As for me, I'm one of those people who chose a different path, a life apart from my parents. It isn't disrespect, it's different wants, desires and dreams.'

'That's a very artful summation. You must have attended a good school.'

'The Valeron school of learning,' he said with a wink. 'Mom and my two aunts were our teachers growing up. They teach for eight months of the year, and most of the kids help with the work during the warmer months. Reading, writing, math and history. Plus, we have a church in town so we learn scripture and worship on Sundays.'

Desiree sighed wistfully. 'Sounds like a heavenly place to live and grow up.'

'I'll probably move back home one day to settle down, once I've sewn the wild seeds of my ambitions.'

She laughed. 'I've wondered how I could ever explain to my parents what I've been doing. With your permission,

I'll steal that line. Next time they ask me why I'm a Pinkerton Eye instead of a dutiful housewife and mother, I'll tell them *I'm sewing the wild seeds of my ambitions!*'

He grinned at her remark. 'I'll picket the horses and give them a little water. Hopefully we'll cross a stream tomorrow so they can drink their fill.'

Desiree gave a bob of her head. 'While you're doing that, I'll lay out the beds and gather some wood for a fire. I have to tell you, I'm famished.'

'Sure you don't want to sleep in the carriage?' he queried a second time. 'Might be a curious snake or scorpion on the prowl during the night.'

She gave him an odd look. 'You aren't comfortable sleeping next to me, are you?'

The assertion wasn't formed like a question. Brett knew a lie would be the worst reply he could give. At his hesitation, she added a curt, 'Well?'

'Miss Moore, I was raised to respect honesty in pretty much every situation.'

He lifted his shoulders in a helpless gesture. 'The truth is, you're about the prettiest gal I ever set eyes on — smart and sweet as honeycomb, too. I didn't get fifteen minutes of sleep lying next to you last night.'

'Why on earth not?' she queried. 'You're not smitten with me, are you?'

'If you have ever taken a good look in a mirror, you are undoubtedly aware that you're a cut above the ordinary. Any man in the country, not blind as a post, would surely regard you as being about as special as a rose blooming in winter.'

To Brett's surprise, the girl's cheeks darkened with embarrassment. She looked at her hands, clasped in her lap, and didn't speak for a few moments. When she finally broke the silence, there was a disheartened inflection in her voice.

'I never wanted to be admired for my looks,' she murmured. 'I always endeavored to be recognized for the person I am, for what I accomplish in deeds.'

'That's why you keep your hair pulled back and wear a Quaker-like bonnet to hide your face.'

'I just . . . '

'You needn't explain yourself,' Brett tried to break the tension of the situation. 'Valeron boys are raised to honor womanhood. I respect you because you're a female and a lady . . . unless you prove otherwise. Beyond that, I can't help the fact that I find you incredibly attractive.'

There was a short, strained silence. Finally, Desiree sighed in resignation. 'I do believe I will sleep in the buggy. I'm not comfortable with the idea of an insect or snake crawling into bed with me.'

'I believe we'll both sleep better that way,' Brett agreed, both relieved and disappointed.

★　★　★

It was mid-morning when the Valeron party spotted a wagon some distance

98

away. Not so large as a Prairie Schooner, it appeared to be a regular buckboard that had been converted into a covered wagon. It was lying on its side, missing a wheel, and no horses were in sight.

'Might be someone who left the wagon behind,' Jared spoke to Wyatt, who was at his side.

Shane and Cliff moved up to either side to see what they were looking at.

'Better take a look,' Wyatt suggested. 'It appears the wagon came down the bank and flipped.'

The four of them proceeded forward, scanning the broken terrain cautiously, uncertain as to what to expect. After a short approach, something that looked like a rifle barrel suddenly appeared, pointing in their direction. Rather than break for cover, they stopped.

'Hello, the wagon!' Jared called. 'Do you need some help?'

'We mean you no harm,' Shane spoke up as well.

After a short pause the rifle barrel

lowered. A moment later, a small head appeared. A little girl of perhaps six or seven years of age appeared. Probably not more than forty pounds, she was very slender, with a tiny pixie face and large eyes. At that moment, it was obvious there had been no rifle, only a short stick that looked like one.

She pointed to the inside of the wagon. 'Mam!' was the only word she said.

The four rode over to the wagon and Cliff was the first to get down. He hurried to the rear of the wagon and peered inside.

'There's a woman in here — a nun!' he said over his shoulder. 'Looks as if she might be injured.'

Jared, pushed by Cliff, shot a single glance at the child, then moved over and knelt down next to the woman. Covered with a blanket, her ashen complexion was worrisome. He spoke to her softly.

The nun's eyes opened to narrow slits, before straining to focus on the man at her side. Her hair had slipped from beneath her veil. It was gray and the wrinkles in her face denoted advanced age. Wyatt had thought to grab his canteen. The young girl refused to drink, so he passed it to Jared. The devote woman managed a few sips and displayed a bit of strength.

'W-who are you?' she asked in a hoarse whisper.

'Jared Valeron and some of my kin, ma'am. We saw your wagon.'

'Two men,' she managed breathlessly. 'They wanted our horse. I tried to get away . . .'

'Yes, ma'am. Looks as if you ended up in a ditch and they got the horse.'

'I was taking Nessy to . . . mission at Santa Fe,' she gasped the words. 'She was Indian hostage.' She coughed and took several breaths. 'Wanted to give her a home.'

'She seems a tad skittish.'

'Only speaks a few words of English.'

'What kind of pain are you feeling?' Jared enquired. 'Can you tell if anything is broken?'

The nun made an effort to smile. 'At my age, everything's broken.'

'Can you tell me anything about the men who robbed you?'

'One was dark skinned . . . quite tall.' She swallowed hard, using the last of her strength to continue. 'The other had a scar . . . side of his nose.'

'Are you hungry?' Jared asked. 'Do you think you could eat something?'

The nun sighed. 'No. You . . . my prayers answered.' Her features grew solemn, a level gaze fixed on Jared's face. 'You will take care of her . . . won't you?'

'Yes, ma'am,' he promised. 'We'll make sure she has a good home.'

She relaxed, expelling a second sigh, heavy and final. She seemed to simply let go of her life, as if she had been staying alive for the single purpose of seeing her charge was in good hands. When her eyes closed, Jared knew they would not open again.

'Mam?' the little girl whispered, crawling over next to Jared.

'She's resting,' Jared told her gently. 'Time for her to join the angels.'

The child's lips pressed tightly together, but she displayed no other emotion. Her blonde hair reached to her shoulders, unkempt presently, but she was fairly clean. The dress had obviously been sewn from a flour sack and she wore no shoes. A lightweight jacket was lying nearby, but her slender arms were bare. She had bright, almost crystalblue eyes and was tan from living out in the open.

Jared tried a few words in Cheyenne and Ute, but she did not reply. Surprisingly, Cliff was the one who reached out to console the child. He placed his hand gently on her shoulder. When she looked at him, he smiled — the same enticing simper he used to charm dozens of innocent girls — and told her, 'Not to worry, dear little Nessy. I'll take care of you. Everything will be all right.'

She glanced quickly at Jared, then back at Cliff.

'You'll see,' Cliff continued his

winning appeal. 'We'll take you home with us. We've got a big house, with lots of kids to play with. You can have your own dog or cat, even a horse to ride. I'll be your big brother and you'll live in a big house with a whole family to love and care for you.'

Nessy might not have understood everything he said, possibly only a few words, but she gave a timid nod of her head. With a delicate hand, she touched her chest, then paced her palm over Cliff's heart, as if she was putting her trust in him.

'Dad-gum.' Jared was awed. 'Your charm works on girls of any age, doesn't it?'

'We need to bury the lady,' Wyatt said softly, squatting at the back of the wagon. 'It would be a sacrilege to drape one of God's servants over the back of a horse.'

'I agree,' Shane said. 'Even if we made up a travois, her body wouldn't last long in this heat. And there's no telling if or when we'll reach any kind of settlement before we get to Brimstone.'

Jared paused to look at Cliff. 'You willing to be the nursemaid for our young guest?'

'I just promised her as much, cousin,' he complained. 'You act like I ain't got a heart.'

'It's just that she's a good ten years from wooing age.'

Cliff sniffed piously. 'I like girls of all ages, not just the ones who follow me around to get attention. She can be the little sister I never had.'

'All right,' Jared declared. 'She's yours to watch over.'

'She'll have to go with us to Brimstone,' Shane put in. 'We've no choice unless we reach a town or mission between here and there.'

'Let's take care of the burial and get moving.' Jared stuck to business. 'The girl can ride double with Cliff. That should give her time to get to know him.'

'Hope that's a good idea,' Shane grinned. 'I started off liking Cliff . . . until I got to know him!'

5

It was late afternoon when Brett drove the buggy up to the front of the Snake Pit establishment. Their arrival did not go unnoticed. Men gathered around before they came to a stop. Brett ignored them, while Desiree, attired in a flattering dress, along with a practical, yet fashionable hat, befitting her cover, gave a slight tip of her head to acknowledge a few of them.

'We were told this was a casino with a stage for entertaining,' Brett spoke to a man standing on the porch. He wore a clean outfit, along with a pair of Colt revolvers. A formidable looking gent, he stood squarely in front of the saloon entrance.

'You sing and dance, do you?' Two-gun asked Brett, displaying a cocky grin.

'I'm more spectator than performer,'

Brett replied easily. 'But my lady boss can make a songbird envious. We've a few days between engagements and thought the saloon owner might pay for a little entertainment.'

'She's a beaut!' said one of the men. 'I'd pay to just look at her.'

'Me, too,' added another.

'We ain't had us any performers since that Shakespeare company come through.' Two-gun snorted his disdain. 'Them people didn't even speak normal words.'

'Can you tell us where to find the boss of this place?' Brett stayed on point.

'I reckon Tynan Dwyer will talk to the lady,' Two-gun said. 'Not so sure about you.'

'The lady is under my protection,' Brett informed the man. 'Until such time as she has her own room and complete privacy, she doesn't go anywhere without me.'

There was a moment where the man facing them seemed to consider if the statement was a challenge. Before he made up his mind, Desiree spoke up.

'For heaven's sake, Brett. If there's going to be a problem with civility or common courtesy in this town, let's keep going. It can't be that far to Santa Fe.'

Two-gun turned his attention to her and quickly removed his hat. 'No, ma'am,' he said quickly. 'We are as pleased as beef in high clover to have you visit our fair town. I was just having some fun with your escort.'

'The last man to have *fun* with my escort ended up in jail with a dent in his skull,' she said testily. 'Please inform the owner of this dubious establishment that we would like to speak to him.'

'Certainly, miss,' he said. 'Denim Montgomery, Enforcer of Brimstone, at your service. If you will both follow me, I'll take you upstairs to see the boss.'

Brett exhaled the breath he'd been holding. He stepped down and gave Desiree a hand. Once at his side, she placed her right hand on his left arm and they fell in behind Montgomery.

Inside the establishment, at the far

end of the saloon, was a stage — five feet higher than the main floor, twenty-five feet across, complete with a full curtain that stretched from wall to wall. An unlit candle-chandelier was centered above the stage, obviously used for lighting.

The rest of the place was rough and masculine, with several paintings hanging on the walls depicting semi-clad females. There were antlers and mounted heads of deer, bear and cougar. The glass on the windows was too dirty to see through, the place reeked of sweat, beer and whiskey, and every man stood up to get a better look at the bedecked lady who had just entered.

Upstairs, they were invited into a large office. Montgomery introduced a man in a suit and a well-dressed lady as Tynan and Lucia Dwyer. Then he left the four of them alone. Brett presented themselves as soon as the door was closed.

'I go by Brett, and this is Desiree Moore,' he said. 'Desiree has the voice of an angel and is available to entertain for the next three nights.'

'A pleasure to have you folks stop in our fair town,' Tynan welcomed them. 'We don't get a great many performers here, being so far off the main trails.'

'It didn't sound as far as it turned out to be,' Brett admitted. 'We were beginning to wonder if we would ever arrive.'

'So you are touring the country?' Lucia asked Desiree.

'Yes. I intended to stay mostly in Colorado, but I received an offer to sing in Santa Fe. I didn't realize the tracks did not go that far yet. A gentleman on the train mentioned there was a town near the border that sometimes hired entertainers.' She laughed her chagrin. 'He didn't say it was — what? — some kind of brigand stronghold?'

Tynan laughed at her description. 'We are a regular municipality,' he assured her. 'You likely noticed we have a bakery, hotel, tavern — everything you would find at any other small town.'

'What type of music do you sing?'

Lucia wanted to know. 'We had an opera singer here one time, but he didn't sing anything in English.'

'Oh, I'm strictly cosmopolitan: songs of the day and a few from days gone by. I sing to entertain, not to impress those with restricted elite or snobbish tastes.'

'And you are willing to sing for three nights?' Tynan asked.

'That would be my limit. We have a schedule to keep.'

'And the pay you require?'

Brett was the one to reply. 'A private room for the lady and $100 for each performance . . . one per night.' At his offer, Desiree laid out the platform.

'I will sing several songs, then step away long enough to have a glass of water. I simply can't sing if my throat is parched. After the short break, I will render a second set and end with a sing-along with the audience, providing we can agree on a tune.' With a tight smile, 'I must tell you, I refuse to indulge in coarse compositions with vulgar or inappropriate lyrics.'

'Sounds wonderful!' Lucia was quick to approve. 'We have a piano player who can play most anything. You only need hum a few bars for him.'

'That's marvelous,' Desiree exclaimed. 'An accompaniment is always welcome.'

'One other stipulation,' Brett announced. 'Miss Desiree does not sit at tables or fraternize with men from the audience. She is a refined and proper lady and is to be treated as such.' He locked gazes with Tynan. 'That must be fully understood by those attending her recital.'

'I'll inform Montgomery,' Tynan promised. 'There will be no trouble.'

'Will you be able to start tonight?' Lucia asked Desiree.

'I need a couple hours to rest up, take a bath and have something to eat.'

'Lucia can see to your needs,' Tynan volunteered. 'Anything you want, you only have to ask.'

'Thank you.'

'What about your escort?' Lucia invited.

'I pretty much take care of myself,'

Brett replied. 'I'll be around whenever Miss Desiree is out and about. As for a bunk, I can sleep most any place.'

'Have Montgomery find you a room,' Tynan ordered. 'He'll make sure you are comfortable.'

Lucia took charge of Desiree, while Brett went downstairs to get her luggage. He found Montgomery waiting for him. After ignoring the man long enough to collect the girl's things, he gave the man a questioning look.

'Mr Dwyer said you would show me where I could sleep while we're here.'

'You always travel with a spare horse?'

Brett grinned. 'Man would be a fool to take a lady on a long journey with only one horse. The second mount is in case of an accident or the draft animal comes up lame.'

'And the saddle?'

'It's my saddle and my horse. If bad came to worse, we could ride double.'

'Been with the lady long?'

'Not that long. She needed a

bodyguard and I happened to be looking for a job.'

'What kind of work did you do prior to meeting her?'

Brett eyed the man up and down. 'Probably one which would have made me unwelcome around this place. I was a bounty hunter.'

Montgomery laughed. 'You don't say?'

'You've probably got fifteen men in town I could collect on, if I hadn't changed professions.'

'Is this a better way of making a living, being the watchdog over some gal?'

'I don't have to sleep on the ground, we eat good, meet nice people and I haven't been shot at once. Yep, it's a whole lot better.' He winked. 'Plus, I get to hear her sing.'

'The lady called you Brett?'

At his nod, Montgomery said. 'OK. I'll take your word you are what and who you say. Don't make the mistake of lying to me. We don't have a lawman in town, but I told you, I'm the enforcer. I keep the peace and don't take kindly to being crossed or lied to.'

'Peace and the joy of music are my only goals these days.'

'See the owner of the tavern. He has an upstairs bedroom where you can stay. He closes early so there's less noise and the hotel is always full. It beats one of the bunk-houses. That's nothing more than a couple rooms with twenty bunk beds and no privacy.'

'How come the tavern owner has a room available?'

'Rules,' he replied. 'The couple running the place need their sleep, so they don't allow drinking, noise, or company after hours.'

'Suits me fine. I won't have much time of my own. Watching over Desiree is a full-time job.'

Montgomery's lips curled and a light danced in his eyes. 'Keeping company with a gal like that doesn't sound much like work to me.'

'No,' Brett allowed, grinning. 'But it

does mean staying alert. I've had to deal with more than a few amorous sorts or drunks.'

'I'll be around to see that doesn't happen while you're in Brimstone.'

'For that, I'm much obliged,' Brett thanked the man. Then he headed to the saloon, carrying the lady's belongings.

★ ★ ★

During the day's ride, Cliff managed to coax a few words out of Nessy. It took some urging, but he learned the child understood more English than she could speak. Nessy didn't remember what happened to her parents, only something scary one night. After that, she was turned loose at an Indian camp to survive among several other feral children. When the blue-coats arrived, they separated the children to find their homes. No one knew anything about Nessy, so they dropped her at a small church. Mam — as she called the nun — volunteered to take her to a mission that handled orphaned children.

The four men and Nessy stopped for the night and made camp at dusk. Although they had brought extra blankets from the wagon, the little girl made it clear she was sharing a bed with Cliff.

'Remember that old red hound that showed up on our doorstep a couple years back?' Shane remarked, once they were all sitting around and eating the rabbit stew Jared had prepared for supper. 'Ma felt sorry for the stray and gave him some leftovers.'

'I remember,' Jared said. 'It followed her every time she went out to hang laundry or work in the garden. Slept under the window of your folks' bedroom.'

'Poor old mutt only lived about six months, but he knew a soft-touch when he saw one.'

Cliff shook his head at the little girl. 'Don't you listen to them, Nessy. I ain't no soft-touch and you ain't no stray pup.'

Shane continued. 'Just saying, you

might have to keep your word to Veta or one of the other girls you've charmed over the past few months. The little tyke needs a mother.'

'I'm sure Faye, Wanetta or Gwen will be thrilled to take in Nessy as a grand-child. All of their kids are grown now.'

Shane smirked at the notion. 'A grandparent isn't the same as a mother and father.'

'Yeah, well, I don't intend to marry the first girl I meet just so the girl can have a mother. There's enough of you Valerons to care for one extra child.'

'What about tomorrow?' Jared asked. 'I can enter town, pretending to be an outlaw.'

'Your short fuse would get you in a fight before you could look around,' Wyatt said.

'Then the two of us! We could take any four of those outlaws!'

'That would leave about a hundred more to deal with,' Wyatt replied. 'No, I've got a better idea, a much safer idea.'

Jared sighed. 'OK, what is it?'

'I've been thinking about Cliff and his wayward waif,' Wyatt said. Looking at his cousin, he suggested, 'You have a perfect cover to enter the town of Brimstone. The little gal needs shoes, a real dress, hat and such. No one will suspect you are looking for Scarlet.'

'Could work,' Jared admitted. 'I doubt anyone would challenge him with Nessy along.'

Cliff, usually with the grin or caustic wit, gazed at his cousins. This was his chance to prove his worth, but it was a direful prospect. He cocked his head and looked at the little girl. She met his stare with a quiet calm, as if she hadn't the slightest interest in a word that had been said.

'I hate the idea of putting Nessy in any danger,' he finally spoke.

'Shouldn't be any,' Wyatt pointed out. 'You don't have to search the town looking for Scarlet. In fact, you only need to keep your eyes open while you buy a handful of supplies and see if they sell some clothes for a child. We don't need an exact count of men with guns, but we do need to know if there are sentries, patrols, guards at the edge of town . . . that sort of thing.'

'That's right,' Jared said. 'Come time for us to search, we'll have a plan based on what you can tell us. We want to be ready to act when Reese and Brett show up.'

'Sure,' Cliff feigned confidence. 'Nessy and I will scout the place.'

'Just remember to keep out of trouble,' Shane chipped in.

'Trust me,' Cliff flashed his customary smirk. 'I got this covered.'

★　★　★

Piano Man was the title the gent went by. He had an ear for music and it took only about ten minutes before he and Desiree were able to get together on her songs. Lucia had not exaggerated, he could play the chords to about anything, whether he had heard it before or not. His location next to the stage was convenient, so he didn't have to move from his usual spot.

When the time for the performance came, the big chandelier was lit and Piano Man hit a few loud introduction keys. Tynan took the stage and raised his hands to quiet the crowd. Word had spread about a guest singer and a full house was in attendance. Many were standing along the walls or lined up against the staircase.

'A special treat for everyone tonight,' Tynan said. 'Let's welcome the song-stress who will entertain us this evening . . . Miss Desiree Moore!'

Desiree came out from behind the curtain to noisy applause and a good many shouts. She had a fixed smile on her face, but Brett could see the nervousness in her eyes. This was not a gathering for a Sunday meeting or wedding. These were mostly wanted men, with crimes ranging from simple theft to the most heinous acts imagin-able. Thankfully, the few storekeepers or others who worked in Brimstone were also there, some with their wives and children.

Piano Man played a familiar strain for an intro and then Desiree lifted a melody to fill the room. She had a beautiful voice, a moderate soprano, yet able to hit the higher notes of an opera singer. The first tune was short and lively to get everyone's attention. Then she demonstrated her softness and range with a canorous rendition of 'Silver Threads Among the Gold'.

Brett was so enthralled by her music he had to remind himself to look around. It was unlikely a prisoner like Scarlet would be allowed to attend the show. Even so, Brett scanned the crowded floor covertly and searched near the upstairs. A woman was there, but it was Tynan's lovely wife, Lucia. Shifting his glance, Brett finally spotted a person of interest. He was a clean-shaven man, wearing a fancy black leather vest, over a black shirt. His hat was also black with a wide silver hatband, and he wore a matched set of pistols with pearl-handled grips. The fellow fit the description of the Waco Kid. If the man who identified Waco in Pueblo, Colorado, was correct, then Brett was at the right place. Scarlet must be within the confines of Brimstone. The task was to find out where they were keeping her.

Desiree ended her performance by asking those who knew the words to join in, singing the 'Sweet By and By'. As the tune ended, she stepped back and curtsied. The room exploded with a thunderous ovation. She reached out with her arms as if to thank each customer, ducked her head in a final salutatory nod, and then disappeared behind the curtain.

Brett moved quickly to prevent anyone from going backstage. His effort was unnecessary, as Denim Montgomery was already in place at the foot of the short staircase. His presence alone kept the men corralled on the main floor.

Brett paused when he reached his side

and said, 'I congratulate you, Montgomery. You seem to have the respect of this very tough crowd.'

The enforcer smiled. 'We have to keep order or this rabble would burn the whole town to the ground just for fun. Everyone knows the rules, and Tynan introduced your lady boss himself. That carries a lot of weight.'

'What did you think of her singing?'

The man stared, unseeing for a moment. 'It reminded me of a time, once when I was still young and respectable. I escorted a proper lady to one of them operas. Didn't care for much of the story, but there was a song or two . . . ' He didn't have to finish.

'Yes, Desiree may one day sing in such a theater.'

Montgomery snorted his disdain. 'Be a waste of talent. Why please a few high-faluting snobs when you have the knack to tame a room of wild men? She should share her gift with audiences like these, people who really appreciate her talent.'

'I'll pass along your thoughts.'

He laughed. 'Damn. I haven't talked in such a way in years.'

'Music can do that to a man.'

Montgomery returned to his job. 'Soon as the lady is ready, I'll clear a path to the stairway.'

'We'll be along without delay.'

The words were barely out of his mouth when Desiree appeared at the steps leading to or from backstage. Brett moved to take her arm as the enforcer of Brimstone began to clear the way. He had designated certain men to keep the others back, providing a stern and respected presence. The pathway was a full six feet wide all the way to the staircase.

Before going upstairs, Desiree paused to place a delicate hand on his arm and smiled at the man for his assistance.

'Thank you so much, Mr Montgomery,' she said in a serious voice. 'It is often more than a single escort can manage to clear the passage for me. I do appreciate a show of affection or appreciation, but I don't enjoy being manhandled or mauled when I leave the stage.'

'My pleasure, Miss Desiree,' Montgomery said, obviously beguiled by her smile. 'During your stay, whenever you wish an additional escort, I'll join you and Brett. Any time or any place.'

She rewarded him with a second simper. 'Thank you again. We may take advantage of your generous offer.'

Then she and Brett made their way up to the second floor and went down the hallway to her door. There was a man in the corridor, sitting at the far end of the hall, reading a book.

'Always someone up here watching,' Brett said under his breath.

'Yes, and the door at the end of the hall appears to be bolted from the outside.'

'Could be used as a jail cell.'

'Or to house an unwilling guest,' Desiree whispered. 'Lucia took in a full bucket of water and towels before I went down for the show. She seemed uneasy when I saw her with the items.'

'I spotted Waco among the crowd. If the information from my father was correct, the outlaw's presence means my sister is here.'

'I didn't get a chance to look for the two wanted men I'm after. The light was too bright on the stage and the faces were all a blur because of the size of the crowd.'

'Might I say, you were a total success. You're not only the most beautiful woman I ever worked with, but you have a splendid voice.'

Desiree's lips parted in a slender smile. It was not as bright as the one she had put on for the show, it was more personal . . . intimate even. Gazing into her chromatic green eyes, Brett was transfixed, impulsively drawn closer . . . closer . . .

'Brett!' the lady gasped softly. 'We're not alone!'

Startled, his senses rebounded at once. He stepped back a full step and made a quick recovery. 'Yes, Miss

Moore,' he said, loud enough to carry. 'I'll be here to escort you to breakfast.'

'Thank you, Brett,' she responded politely, but a revealing pink hue imbued her cheeks.

As the door closed, he wondered if she had felt the same impulse to kiss him, or had he simply embarrassed her?

Ain't no time for romancing, Bonehead, he scolded himself. You've near a hundred gunmen watching your every move. One mistake and you'll be singing, too — in a heavenly choir.

6

'What do you think?' Wyatt asked Jared, as Cliff and Nessy started off towards town.

'I rode as far as the valley at daylight and took a look. The town is located at an old waterhole. It's pretty much open at either end, with slight rolling hills to one side and a small range of mountains and the spring to the other.'

Wyatt queried, 'How about patrols or sentries?'

'I didn't dare get too close. The town has a bunch of wagons and tents, plus a couple of large structures — looked like rooming houses. There's other buildings and a two-storey affair, probably the main saloon. At the outskirts, I saw a couple horses and their riders,' Jared postulated. 'They didn't appear to be camped out, but I'd guess they were keeping an eye for anyone headed their way. Probably another pair at the other end, too. Be real tricky to enter from either side, being that it's a choppy range of hills over here and a wide expanse of open ground for a mile on the far side.'

'You and I will use the cover of the hills and take another look later this morning,' Wyatt said. 'We need to draw a sketch of the buildings and hope Cliff can remember which is which. Come time to act — providing Scarlet is there — we will need all of the information we can get.'

'Another thing, Wyatt, we need to get eyes over at the east end of town. If Reese or Brett come by train, they will come up from that direction.'

'Shane can head over there,' Wyatt suggested. 'Wouldn't do for our kin to walk into trouble, before we could warn them. If they did come by train, they could be arriving at any time.'

Wyatt called Shane over. He had been tethering the horses where they could get a little grass. It was slim pickings around the hills, but the animals could also get a little from the sage and scrub brush. The three of them talked over the options and Shane took the freshest mount and headed through the hills. He would be far enough away from town to avoid being seen and make his way a mile or so beyond Brimstone before turning toward the railroad. He packed enough food for the day and would return in time to be in camp by dark.

'I hate every second we delay going in after Scarlet,' Jared anguished, as Shane rode off. 'I know we have to have a plan, but . . . '

He left the statement hanging and Wyatt added, 'We would be no good to her dead, cousin. You know your sister wouldn't want any of us to get killed trying to save her.'

'If anyone has touched her . . . ' Jared groaned at the notion, then set his teeth. 'I'll rip the beating hearts out of every one of them kidnappers and squash it under my heel.'

'Don't know where you got your temper,' Wyatt remarked. 'Good thing some of us came along who are willing to use our heads.'

'If I had your speed with a gun, I'd have gone in alone.'

'You're a hunter, Jer. For me, shooting is the only thing I ever enjoyed. I've always been consumed by shooting any kind of gun at any kind of target.' He heaved a breath, as if his memory and conscience were in conflict. 'I wanted to do something big, be the hero of the stories we had heard growing up. Jim Bridger, Daniel Boone, Davy Crockett. I wanted one day to have Wyatt Valeron added to that list.'

'More likely you'll end up as just another name in the graveyard.'

'Thanks,' Wyatt said dryly.

'If you want, I'll make up a nice headstone for you: *Here lies Wyatt Valeron — not as fast as he thought!*'

'Next to it, you can have your own,' Wyatt fired back. '*Jared Valeron, killed because he didn't know when to shut up!*'

Jared laughed. 'OK, let's get the

horses saddled.'

'With you all the way, cousin,' Wyatt replied. 'At least as far as the cemetery.'

★ ★ ★

Desiree and Brett made use of the dining room at the Hash House. The couple running the place were middle-aged, and there were two Indian women working as servers. Nothing fancy, the meals offered were listed on a sign — One, Two or Three — with the items included and price for each. It appeared they had made up three posters — one each for breakfast, lunch and dinner.

'Number Three looks good,' Desiree said to Brett, once they had sat down at a reasonably clean table. 'Eggs, toast, potatoes and ham.'

Brett addressed a stone-faced Indian woman. 'Two of the Number Three specials.'

Without a reply, the woman turned about and waddled over toward the kitchen. A youngster of about fourteen was going table to table with a pot of coffee. As he reached them, he grinned at Desiree.

'You sure do sing pretty, ma'am,' he gushed awkwardly. 'We got some milk in the back, if'n you want some in your coffee?'

She thanked him, flashing one of her smiles. 'Have you some sugar, too?'

'Yes'um, we do. I'll bring some out straight away.'

As he hurried off, Desiree shook her head. 'Wonder how he and the Indians ended up here?'

'His folks likely had debt problems. The squaws might have been married to hunters or miners at one time or another. If they've no place else to go, this work would keep them from starving or ending up on a reservation.'

'So not everyone is a bandit, murderer or thief here.'

'I talked to a few men last night,' Brett informed her. 'The business owners are mostly down on their luck people. Tynan hired people to run the bakery, general store, tavern and the like. There's even a dozen or so children in town.'

'I saw a few of those in the audience.'

The youth returned with a beaker of milk and small tin of sugar. Before Desiree had her coffee flavored to her taste, the meal arrived. She thanked the boy and the next few minutes were spent eating a passable meal. They were nearly finished when Brett noticed a ruckus out on the street. He caught a glimpse of one of the men and straightened up.

'Stay here,' he cautioned. 'I'll have a look and see what's going on.'

Without waiting for her response, Brett rose from the table and hurried outside.

Three men were in a tussle — two against one — and the lone man was Cliff Mason! Brett raced outside as a little girl grabbed hold of one man's leg and sank her teeth into his thigh. He howled in pain and raised an arm, ready to bat her away.

Brett leapt forward and blocked his

swing. The girl let go as Brett hammered the man with a solid punch to the side of his head, hard enough that it knocked him off his feet.

Cliff was losing his match against the second assailant, but Denim Montgomery arrived before Brett had a chance to lend him a hand.

'Everyone hold it!' he snarled. 'Next man who throws a punch will answer to me!'

Brett stepped back as Cliff got up from the ground and dusted himself off. The little girl flew over to hug him about the waist, looking fearfully at the circle of men.

'You!' Montgomery demanded of Brett. 'What's going on?'

'I haven't the slightest idea,' Brett replied. 'The joker sitting in the dirt raised his hand to strike the little girl. I don't stand by while anyone mistreats a child.'

Rather than speak to any of the others, Montgomery knelt down next to the child and offered her a gentle smile.

'Will you talk to me, little darlin'?' he said, his voice soft and coaxing. 'What started this here fracas?'

'Hurt . . . Mam,' she whimpered, pointing at the two men. 'Them. Hurt Mam.'

'Mam is what she called the elderly nun who was taking her to an orphan mission,' Cliff clarified. When Montgomery gave him the go ahead to explain, he told how he had found the nun and little girl in an overturned wagon. He related how the two men had stolen their horse and supplies, then left them both to die in the desert.

'That ain't how it happened a'tall!' the man Brett had knocked down declared. 'Pip's horse came up lame; we only wanted the horse.'

'Clay's telling it true,' Pip whined. 'The church gal tried to get away and ran off the trail. We didn't figure she was hurt none.'

'Too busy robbing them to check, huh?' Montgomery barked the words. 'I suppose you didn't think about the little girl, either. Didn't stop to think you were stranding a woman and child fifty miles away from the nearest help.'

'Hey!' Clay argued. 'This here feller came along, didn't he?'

Cliff did not hide his contempt. 'I'd ridden for two days and never seen a soul on that old trail. The child would have died too if I hadn't been riding cross-country to reach the main road.'

'Why come to Brimstone?' Montgomery asked him.

'Look at this poor little nipper!' he explained. 'She ain't got a thing to wear but that flour-sack dress. I come here because she needs shoes and clothes. We also need enough supplies so I can get her to a mission.'

Montgomery selected several men. 'Landau, Sike, Elmo. You three take these two nun-killers over to the shed. I'll tell the boss about this and we'll set up a hearing.'

'I'll make ready with a couple ropes,' Elmo sneered. 'I ain't a religious man, but my ma was.'

The three appointees disarmed and led the two men away, both of them still professing innocence of any wrong-doing. Montgomery had remained on one knee. He smiled at the little girl.

'Don't you worry about those bad men,' he told her kindly. 'They won't bother you again.'

The girl raised her head enough to make eye contact. She didn't actually smile, but she seemed to understand and displayed a measure of relief.

'Break it up,' Montgomery ordered the remaining spectators, as he rose to his feet. 'Excitement is over.'

Brett hesitated just long enough for Cliff to turn his direction.

'Much obliged,' Cliff said. 'Me and Nessy were a little over-matched.'

Brett grinned. 'Nessy was holding her own. You're the one who was getting the stuffing beaten out of you.'

Brett nodded toward the cafe. 'If you two need some breakfast, we'd be happy to buy a meal for the both of you.' He put his hand on Nessy's shoulder. 'You hungry, sweetheart? Want something to eat?'

'Uh-huh,' she said.

'You're welcome to join us too, Montgomery,' Brett offered the town enforcer. 'We've about finished, but — '

'I already ate,' he cut off the invite. 'Thanks anyway.'

Cliff paused before heading into the eating house and directed his question at Montgomery. 'You gonna need me to stick around for the hearing?'

'Wouldn't hurt,' he replied. 'I 'spect we'll get to it right after lunch. I don't think we'll need a lot of testimony, so it should be a quick judgment and a quicker hanging.'

Cliff's eyebrows peaked. 'Whoa! You don't mess around in this town.'

'Them two coyotes have been looting and murdering for years. Killing a nun, even by accident, is going to close the book on their worthless lives.'

'I see why you are able to keep order in a lawless town like this,' Brett remarked.

'See you fellows later,' Montgomery

said. Then he walked off down the street.

Cliff picked up Nessy and her tiny arms slipped about his neck. He gave a sheepish look as Brett displayed curiosity at her fond attachment. Once they had joined Desiree at their table, Brett introduced them to her. Nessy pointed at an item or two on one of the nearby tables, so Cliff knew what to order for her. Desiree also acquired a glass of milk from the boy who attended to the coffee.

After the two of them were served and eating, Brett leaned over next to Desiree and whispered that Cliff was his cousin. Her eyes broadened at the news and she took a closer look at the little girl.

'If you came for Brett's sister, how did you end up with the stray lamb?'

'Exactly as I told the crowd, miss,' he related in a lowered voice, 'except for the part about being alone. There's three Valeron boys a couple miles outside of town. Me and Nessy came in to reconnoiter and try to determine if Scarlet is here.'

'We're pretty sure she is,' Brett advised him. 'I spotted the Waco Kid, and he was identified as one of the kidnappers.'

'And you?' Cliff beamed a seductive smile at Desiree. 'What's a lovely young lady such as yourself doing way out here?'

'I'm looking for a couple bandits who held up a train a few months back.'

'She's a Pinkerton agent,' Brett informed him quietly.

'Boy, Hannah!' Cliff did not hide his shock. 'You don't say!'

'What did you see on the ride in?' Brett got down to business. 'How many guards?'

'Only a couple at the outskirts of town, but everyone in this stronghold might stand against us when we try and steal your sister back. Tell you straight, I never seen so many plug-ugly gunnies in one place. Jared and Wyatt figured I ought to look around, being that I'm the least likely guy to suspect. Having a little girl was supposed to be a perfect cover.'

'Why did you pick a fight with the two guys and risk exposure?' Desiree wanted to know.

Cliff scoffed at the suggestion. 'I didn't pick the fight. When Nessy saw the two men, she began to shout: *Men hurt Mam! Men hurt Mam!* They wanted to shut her up.'

'Seems like she doesn't speak much English.'

'Only a few words. I don't know how long the Indians had her, but she forgot most everything she knew. Poor kid, left all alone in the world, suffering at the hands of a band of savages,' he sighed. 'It's why I told her she could come with us. I kind of promised to take care of her.'

'You personally?'

His customary grin surfaced. 'Well, I invited her to join the family. I mean, there are plenty of Valerons and other kinfolk at the ranch. She can join in with the other kids on the ranch and recoup a little of what she's lost.'

'Funny,' Brett said, 'but I always figured you for a skirt-chasing lout who would one day get killed by an angry husband, relative, or jealous paramour. And here you are befriending a little lost waif. Maybe I misjudged you.'

'That's a lame way to pay a man a compliment.'

Brett chuckled. 'I still wouldn't trust you alone with any of my female kin, nor Desiree, either.'

Desiree smiled at the playful exchange. 'I'm not incapable of evaluating whether a man is a gentleman or a louse.' When Cliff had no reply, she stated the obvious about their mission. 'You can't believe the five of you can take on the whole town. Is there more help coming?'

'Reese will probably be arriving at any time,' he responded. 'Jared expects him to bring a couple of men. Your father asked him to pick up someone named RJ from Cheyenne.'

'RJ?' Brett repeated. 'Don't know who that is.'

'No matter. Once he shows, we are going to decide on a plan.'

'OK. I'll slip out tonight so we can coordinate a rescue attempt. With Desiree being upstairs, close to where we think Scarlet is, we should be able to get to her quickly. We only have to figure a way out before we're discovered.'

'The plan might be a little more difficult than that,' Desiree interjected coyly. 'I just spotted the two men I came looking for.'

'She's on the level?' Cliff queried. 'Now we're supposed to rescue your sister, grab several kidnappers, and also snag a couple bandits for the Pinkertons?'

'The lady is part of our team,' Brett informed him. 'We do this by priorities. First, we rescue Scarlet. Second, if we can manage it, we grab the kidnappers. And third, we pick up the two bandits.'

Cliff laughed. 'Well, sure, when you explain it like that, this should be a cake walk.'

*　★　★

Tynan listened to Montgomery's report, while sitting idly behind his desk. When the man finished, he rose to his feet and paced slowly about the room. After a second complete circle he came to a stop.

'You say Brett came to the man's aid?'

'Actually, he jumped in when one of the pair was about to strike the little girl. Guess she had rushed in to help that Mason fella and bit one of the thugs on the leg.'

'And now the four of them are having breakfast together at Cookie's place?'

'Brett made the offer when he learned the little girl was an orphan. Seemed a polite thing to do.' He hurried to add, 'He also invited me.'

Tynan wished Denim had accepted the offer. He had a bad feeling and it continued to grow worse daily, the worry that an army of Valeron men would swoop down and destroy his town. As far as Brett joining in a fight to protect a child, that was something any decent man would have done, but this was a dangerous time to trust anyone.

'Tell Brett and this Mason fellow that I want them at the trial . . . in case I have any questions.'

'I already told the guy and his orphan to stick around.'

'We'll have the hearing one hour from now, downstairs, before the place fills up for the day.'

'Whatever you say, boss.'

'Keep the hearing to a handful of men, no more than twenty or so. Ricky and Elmo can handle the hanging. Everyone who wants to see that is welcome to watch.'

'I'll have Waco man the door. He can pick and choose the men who attend the hearing so's you can pick a jury if you want one.'

'That should be fine,' Tynan approved. 'Make certain you have a couple of the more reliable guns handy, in case there's any trouble.'

'We expecting some?'

'No, but I like to be prepared for any contingency.'

Montgomery grinned. 'Ain't sure what that word *contingency* means, but I'll see we're ready for it or anything else.'

'Good man, Denim. Once those two are hanged, you can take charge of the bodies and claim whatever reward there is on their heads.'

'Right,' Montgomery replied. 'I'll get things organized.'

As he left the office, Tynan followed him to the hallway. He asked the guard about Lucia and he motioned she was in with Scarlet. Before he could decide on an action, Lucia came out with a partially empty plate and glass. She hurried up to where he was, always eager to do his bidding. He enjoyed that about her, the way she sought to constantly please him. In return, he had tried to give her everything she wanted.

'You need something, dear?' she asked.

He noticed the food had barely been touched and the glass had a white film.

'The girl drinks milk instead of coffee?'

Lucia smiled. 'Doesn't like coffee, but is used to having milk with her meals. That's probably good for her, because she doesn't eat much. I believe she has lost a couple pounds since she arrived. The two gowns I gave her don't fit too well. With her being three or four inches taller than me and her slender build, they hang on her like rags. Maybe I should go over to the store and see if I can find something closer to her size.'

Tynan waited patiently while Lucia rattled on. She would often get preoccupied with something and he had to wait until she was finished to change her train of thought. He gave a nod of approval concerning her idea for a dress, then explained what he had in mind.

'How can we do this without letting the visitors see her?' she asked.

'Have her wear that black lace dress of yours, the one with the veil.'

She bobbed her head in comprehension. 'Yes, that should work.'

'I'll send Landau up. He will be at her side and warn her to keep quiet. Besides that, I am controlling the number of people who attend the trial.'

'And I'm to watch Scarlet for any sign of recognition?'

'Yes. You can tell her we are allowing her to see how we keep the peace in Brimstone and what kind of life she can expect. It will appear as if we are trying to induct her into our world. While she is observing the hearing, watch the girl carefully. Landau will survey the four people below. I don't think we need doubt the little girl, but one of those two men could be a Valeron,' he harrumphed. 'Even the singer. Who knows how they will enter town, should they find us.'

'I'll keep a close eye on Scarlet for any sign of recognition,' Lucia promised.

'Thank you, my love.'

Lucia appeared to chew her lip. Tynan constituted from her nervous habit that she had something more to add and asked, 'Yes?'

'Your brother made a terrible mistake in bringing the Valeron girl here. He has jeopardized everything we've worked for these past few years. Can't we send her back home?'

'Her groom was killed during the kidnapping. Even if we managed to return the girl, there's no guarantee the Valerons would not come looking for retribution. Wyatt Valeron is one man Waco would not be eager to test his skill against with a gun. Plus, they have a U.S. Marshal in the family, too.'

Lucia had to reach around him with a plate in one hand and the empty glass in the other, but she moved in close to Tynan, wanting to feel his arms around her. She had always been affectionate, ever since their relationship blossomed into the love they now shared.

'I'm afraid,' she murmured. 'I don't want to lose the life we have together.'

Tynan kissed her. 'I won't let that happen,' he whispered into her ear. 'I promise.'

7

Desiree was next to Brett, and Cliff held Nessy in his arms. A few feet away, Montgomery and another capable-looking man had control of the two prisoners. The tall one, Pip, was openly defiant, while the one with the scar on his nose, Clay, looked mostly at his feet.

'You men are charged with the killing of a nun and leaving this young orphan to die in the wilderness,' Tynan accused the pair. 'You can speak if you've a mind to.'

'It was an accident,' Pip spoke up. 'Clay's hoss come up lame. We only wanted their gelding. But the old gal struck at me with her whip and skedaddled off down the trail. She's the one who run off into the ditch and got herself busted up.'

'Then you took their supplies and

their horse,' Tynan continued with the charges.

'There was nuthen we could do for the old gal. She done broke her neck or something and couldn't move. As for the brat, she growled and hissed at us like some kind of blasted she-cat!'

'So you left the two of them stranded in the middle of nowhere,' Tynan concluded.

Brett saw that the acting judge seemed to have eyes for something other than the two criminals. He glanced up at the upstairs balcony and saw three shadowy figures — Lucia, a gunman, and another female. That girl was wearing a black dress, like that of a Spanish dancer, and a veil to cover her face. Even hidden, he knew in an instant it was Scarlet. She had a way of standing that was as erect as a statue. Add to that, her hands were clasped together at her waist, holding a dark wrap . . . possibly to conceal that her wrists were bound.

He kept his own eyes roving, knowing that any recognition would give himself away. Cliff had not noticed the trio, as his eyes were on the judge and the two men. Brett remained casual, indifferent to everything but the court proceedings.

'I find you both guilty,' Tynan announced his verdict. 'You will be taken to the gallows at the far end of town and hanged. Any last words?'

'It was an accident!' Pip cried. 'You can't hang us for a nun dying by accident!'

'Maybe not,' Tynan volleyed back. 'But you did admit to stealing a horse. The sentence for horse-thieving in these parts is death by hanging!'

The two men were herded out of the room and most of the spectators followed. Montgomery stayed behind with Cliff and the others. He grinned at Brett, once the place had cleared out.

'Justice is served,' he said.

'Quick and to the point,' Brett displayed his support. He then glanced at Cliff. 'Are you satisfied with the sentence, Mr Mason?'

Cliff gave a bob of his head. 'I hope that knowing those bad men are gone will help Nessy to sleep. I've had to cuddle her close and reassure her the past couple nights because of bad dreams.'

Desiree glanced up and saw that the trio on the upstairs landing had begun to move back to the hallway. She asked Montgomery, 'Who is the lady with the veil? Someone special?'

Brett just about swallowed his teeth, but masked his shock at once. Cliff had never even seen the woman referred to, so he merely put on a curious look for Montgomery.

The enforcer was matter-of-fact. 'We get a guest now and then who don't want their identities known. We've had a state senator staying here for a while once. Another time, a judge who made an unpopular decision concerning a trial visited our fair town until tempers cooled. Crooked bankers, adulterers, sinners of all kinds, come here for sanctuary.'

'I see.' Desiree was distinctively innocent. 'Perhaps, should I ever be chased by a possessive admirer, I will return here to escape from him.'

Montgomery grinned. 'You will always be welcome, Miss Desiree.'

★　★　★

Tynan cornered Landau in the hallway and gestured to Lucia to come to his office. Once they were inside, he put anxious eyes on them.

'Well?'

'I wouldn't want to play poker against the lady,' Landau said. 'She never flinched or gave any indication that she knew anyone downstairs.'

'She had the veil to hide behind,' Lucia added, 'but I also detected nothing. She showed no interest in anything but the child and the trial itself.'

Tynan allowed a breath to escape noisily. 'That's a relief.'

'I did see the singer's bodyguard take a look at us,' Landau remarked, 'but it was more casual than curious. It was the same alertness he has shone since he arrived. Man takes his job seriously.'

'Ex-bounty hunter is his claim.'

Landau nodded. 'Yeah? He looks capable.'

'Good job,' Tynan praised them both. 'I didn't want to take any chances.'

'You've still got a problem,' Landau said. 'Dillon got drunk last night and started talking about taking over the leadership here in town. He wanted to come take the girl and dethrone you and Lucia. Montgomery showed up and he backed off some, but I think a challenge is coming.'

'This is all because of that blasted woman!' Tynan cried.

'Miss Valeron has sworn that she will never submit to him, Tynan,' Lucia said quietly. 'I see a strength of resolve in her; she will die before she allows Dillon to touch her.'

'And I can't abide any man taking a genteel woman by force,' Landau professed. 'I'm sorry, boss. Brother or no, I won't let that happen.'

Tynan rubbed his temples. Dillon caused more headaches than a temperance rally invading a drinking contest.

'There are a good many arranged marriages in this country,' he attempted to defend Dillon's notion. 'Why should this be any different?'

'It's different because of who and what she is!' Landau declared. 'If it means a fight, so be it!'

'Damn, Landau!' Tynan cried. 'I'm between the branding iron and the fire. Dillon has enough men on his side to start a war against me. There must be some way to convince Scarlet to accept him as her husband.'

'Maybe,' Lucia put in, 'once she knows her family isn't coming, she might change her mind.'

'That could take months. Dillon isn't going to wait that long.'

Landau tipped his hat to Lucia and backed to the door. 'You know my position on this, boss. I'm on your side, but I'll stand up for the lady.'

The door closed after him and Tynan stared helplessly at Lucia. 'What am I supposed to do?'

'Dillon broke the rules on this raid

— he killed a man and kidnapped an innocent woman.'

Tynan shook his head. 'Is there anything we can say or do to make Scarlet accept Dillon as her husband?'

'No.' Lucia sighed, wishing she could offer hope, but knowing this was a wasted conversation. 'I suppose, if no one shows up to rescue her, she might decide to make the best of her situation. However, it will never be your brother. She hates him.'

★　★　★

Cliff and Nessy had purchased what supplies they needed. Brimstone was just out of sight when Nessy grunted for his attention and pointed up the trail ahead. As the two of them continued on, he made out Shane, sitting on the odd-colored mare, the one he called Beauty.

'Tell me true, Nessy,' Cliff said, as they drew closer. 'Have you ever seen a more homely horse in your life?'

'Like Injun pony,' Nessy replied.

'But a whole lot uglier! Even a mustang would run and hide from that hideous cuss.'

Shane waved him toward a brush-laden draw. He and his mount disappeared from sight, so Cliff followed along until he spotted Reese Valeron, sitting atop a buckboard. The wagon bed had a tarp over a pile of goods or supplies, and two capable men from the ranch were sitting on their horses nearby.

Cliff pulled up a short way from the wagon and climbed down. He turned and lifted Nessy off the horse. As she made no effort to be put down, he continued to carry her.

'Hey, Cliff!' Reese greeted him. 'Shane told me that you've been adopted by a little orphan.'

'She knows a good man when she sees one.'

'Yet she still went along with you,' Reese grinned. 'Hi there, Nessy!' he waved. 'Is Cliff taking good care of you?'

'*Daddy*! Not Cliff,' she spouted importantly.

Reese didn't reply to her correction. 'What did you find out? Is Scarlet in town?'

Cliff outlined the situation, from the number of gunmen, to the upstairs rooms, and then filled them in on Brett and Desiree.

'I'm impressed!' Reese exclaimed when he had finished. 'Brett didn't waste any time. How'd he find a singer to go along with his infiltrating the stronghold?'

'She works for the Pinkerton agency. She is after two train robbers in town. She wants us to take them into custody when we grab the half-dozen or so men involved in the kidnapping.'

Reese laughed at the ridiculous notion. 'Isn't it enough that we've got to rescue Scarlet from a town full of law-hating gunmen, and we're supposed to do Pinkerton's job, too?'

Cliff shrugged. 'Don't ask me how this can be done. That's yours and

Brett's baby. He's going to slip out tonight. We're supposed to all meet at the campsite. I told him we would have someone waiting west of town to show him the way.'

'Reb and Dodge can stick here with the wagon for now,' Reese outlined. 'I'll go to the camp with you and wait for Brett to arrive. Tonight, we'll put our heads together and discuss our options.'

'You meet up with RJ, like your pa asked?' Cliff wondered.

Reese chuckled. 'Yeah, RJ was with Nash.'

'The good Doctor Valeron didn't make the trip?'

'He's in the middle of his apprenticeship. If he left, he might lose his spot at the hospital. I told him, if any of us get wounded, we'll try and live long enough to have him treat us.'

Cliff grunted. 'That's real comforting.'

'We've time enough to have something to eat,' Shane spoke up. 'It's a two-hour ride through the hills to the camp, seeing as we have to stay out of sight of the lookouts.' He nodded at Cliff. 'You and Nessy gather up a little smokeless firewood. Make sure you don't pick up anything green.'

'OK,' he said, putting Nessy down and taking her hand. 'Let's get some wood for Shane.'

A slight smile curled on her small pixie face. 'OK, Daddy.'

'Yes, *Daddy*,' Shane teased. 'Better let Nessy show you the best sticks for a fire. She's probably a lot better at gathering firewood than you.'

★　★　★

Desiree pointed out the two train robbers to Brett while they were taking a leisurely stroll over to the bakery. After buying a couple of pastries, they returned to her room. Brett ignored the guard and followed the lady inside. Brett sat on the only chair, while Desiree rested on the edge of her bed.

'What is our plan?' Desiree asked,

once they had finished off the tasty sweet rolls.

'I'll slip out after tonight's performance. I can get by the night patrol easy enough. They will be watching for anyone coming into town, so I'll have to be more careful on my return.'

'Do you think your older brother is here by now?'

'Cliff seemed to think he would arrive today. Reese started out a day behind Jared and the others, but he took the train, same as we did. If he isn't here yet, he will certainly arrive tomorrow. As that will be your last performance, we have to plan something for tomorrow night or first thing the next morning. We don't dare stick around any longer than that.'

The girl chewed her lip and displayed a worrisome expression. 'I don't know, Brett. This place is a fortress, and I've counted nearly a hundred gunmen. How can a mere handful of us rescue your sister, arrest a half dozen men and still escape with our lives?'

'Jared and Wyatt will have an idea or two, and Reese is a smart guy. Cliff will have told them what we're up against, so we will all put our heads together. All we have to do is get in, do the job, and get out in one piece. Then we only have to outrun any pursuit for a hundred miles or so.' He grinned. 'How hard can that be?'

'It's not a priority if we don't arrest my two train robbers.'

'If we can take six ruthless kidnappers, including the brother of the man who runs Brimstone, we ought to be able to grab a couple thieves with no problem.'

Desiree rose from the bed and began to pace the room. 'No, it's impossible,' she complained. 'If we all work together, we might be able to steal Scarlet away from these men, but it's ludicrous to think we can outfox a whole town and capture so many men without the help of the Army.'

Brett had stood up as soon as the girl was on her feet. At her negative statement, he planted himself in her path.

She stopped to keep from running into him and gazed up into his eyes.

'Let's not shoot the horse until we're sure its leg is broken, Desiree. If we can't figure a way to nab the kidnappers and the others, we'll do what is necessary to get Scarlet away safely. We're not going to ride in with guns blazing and get a bunch of people killed — especially my kin.'

'But it's hopeless!'

'Let me see what the guys and I can come up with before you worry yourself sick. You've got to sing for these fellows again tonight. For the time being, that's the only thing you have to worry about.'

The girl inched close enough that she was able to rest her head against Brett's chest. He marveled at the texture and flowery scent of her hair, at the warmth that flooded through him at having her so close. He eased his arms around her until he had enveloped her in a reassuring embrace.

Desiree subtly slipped her arms around Brett. Shortly, she raised her head from his chest, lifting her eyes to meet his. An ungovernable impulse seized hold of his willpower. Before he could summon forth a rationale, Brett found his lips melded with her own. It was the most wondrous sensation he had ever experienced. Not pruriently impassioned, the union was filled with desire, without morphing into sexual desire. It was awe-inspiring, consolatory, and felt as right as breathing.

When they broke contact, he kissed her cheek and held her close. In such a stance, they remained stationary, as if a single word or breath of air might ruin the moment. Desiree chose to turn her head enough for her mouth to touch his once more. It was a reinforcement of affection, removing any doubt he might have harbored as to whether he had taken advantage of her.

★   ★   ★

Tynan was at his desk when Lucia entered the office. A glance told him something was troubling her.

'What's the matter now?' he asked, weary of the seemingly endless problems since Dillon's return.

'Scarlet didn't show a hint of recognition during the trial, but I don't think we can relax.'

'Why do you say that?'

'I did as you suggested and invited her to sit on the balcony for the performance tomorrow night.' He waited and Lucia blurted, 'Scarlet warned that you and I leave town!'

Tynan skewed up a confused look. 'She did what?'

'She seems more convinced than ever that her family will come for her.' Lucia moistened her lips with a tense flick of her tongue. 'She advised me to try and get you to leave — abandon both this town and your brother. The only alternative is if I help her escape. She asked for a horse and a few supplies, enough to make it to the nearest train station.'

He snorted. 'Well, there you are. She's trying to figure a way to escape. Why should she want to save us? If she had seen one of her kinfolk, she wouldn't be trying to talk you into letting her go.'

But Lucia's fears did not abate. 'I think she was trying to save lives, maybe on both sides. She went so far as to say she would not implicate Landau in the warrants issued for her kidnapping. He kept Dillon at bay during their trip and has treated her with courtesy.'

That bit of information did cause Tynan an uneasy feeling. If she was already deciding who would be punished for the kidnapping and murder, she had to be confident of escape or rescue.

'I wonder about the fellow with the little girl — he could be a Valeron scout.'

Lucia argued, 'I don't think he would risk that girl's life. Did you see them together? The poor little orphan clung to him like a frightened puppy. More than that, Denim told me she actually tried to help him when those two killers attacked him on the street.'

'That only leaves Brett.' Tynan rubbed his hands together, thinking hard. 'He said he was a bounty hunter, but he could be one of the Valeron boys.'

'How could he and Desiree have arrived so quickly?' Lucia argued. 'Dillon said no one knew where they went and no one followed them.'

'We've only had the four new arrivals since Dillon returned. Brett strikes me as competent and cool as ice. He could be after Scarlet.'

'Is there any way you can check his story, dear?' Lucia wanted to know.

Tynan mulled over the problem and made his decision. 'I'll have Denim pass the word: everyone staying in Brimstone will be told to take a good look at him by tonight. We'll see if anyone comes forward with any information.'

'If he is recognized, then what?'

'We'll handle it discreetly and without gun-play. If no one points a finger at him, then we only have to stay on alert until after tomorrow's performance. They will be riding out the morning after and we can continue our watch for other strangers.'

Lucia did not look satisfied, but was resolved. 'I wish Dillon had never laid eyes on that girl.'

'Me, too,' Tynan replied. 'He has endangered all of our lives for a woman he'll never have.'

★ ★ ★

Brett and Desiree went through the same routine as the previous night. This time, the balcony at the top of the stairs was off-limits during the performance. Then, when Desiree took the stage, Tynan and Lucia arrived with two chairs to watch the show. Men lined the stairway, but none intruded upon the balcony area. Brett remained near the stairs that led to the area back of the stage and Montgomery was also close by.

However, all was not the same for this performance. Brett noticed a lot of men wormed their way closer to the stage, then would move back to a different location. It might have been an effort on their part to get a closer look at

Desiree, but he felt the eyes of every single one studying him. It was as if they were coming up to take a look at both of them. This examination was more than envy concerning his being the escort of such a beautiful and talented woman. No, they were giving him the once-over for an unknown reason.

After the final applause and bow from Desiree, Brett went quickly backstage. He praised the young lady for her wonderful singing and then paused to give her a short hug.

'Remember the plan,' he whispered in her ear. 'We might need to use the secondary cover.'

She smiled at him as he pulled away, just in time that Montgomery didn't see they had engaged in a short embrace. He showed his usual smile as he waited to accompany her back to her room.

'Like a songbird on a spring morning, Miss Moore,' he applauded her singing. 'Sure am going to miss having you here. Don't know when we ever had any finer entertainment.'

'Thank you,' she answered humbly. 'I never knew there were so many men in Brimstone. I felt sorry for how cramped the quarters were down on the casino floor.'

'Worth any amount of crowding,' he replied. 'You've got the sweetest voice I ever heard.'

'You are too kind, Mr Montgomery.'

Brett hooked his arm through her own and the two of them followed the pathway the town enforcer had cleared. There again was no trouble reaching the stairs. Desiree was cordial, waving or nodding at the men who shouted and called out compliments for her performance. Once at the staircase, Montgomery bid her goodnight and allowed the two of them to go up to her room.

Desiree waited until she was at her door to give Brett an inquisitive look. 'What's happened? Did someone recognize you?'

'I'm not sure, but the calf might have slipped the noose,' he told her. 'Best be ready.'

She glanced down the hall at the constant guard and asked, 'Is this going to prevent you from meeting the others tonight?'

'I hope not,' he replied. 'All the same, be prepared for anything.'

The lady flashed a professional smile, aware of the guard showing interest in their hushed conversation. 'See you for breakfast,' she said in a normal voice. 'Goodnight, Brett.'

As soon as her door closed, Brett took the stairs, left the saloon, and went directly to his room above the tavern. He kept vigil for a few minutes, then shimmied out of the window via a short length of rope. He dropped silently to the ground and, moving like a cat past a sleeping dog, he padded through the dark and headed for a wash at the west end of town.

Thirty minutes later, he had slipped past the two night guards and reached the rendezvous point. Shane was there waiting with two horses. They proceeded to the Valeron camp where Reese, Wyatt and Jared were there to greet him.

'We could be running short of time,' Brett told the men, once they had settled down around a long-since dead fire pit. 'I've been the target of a lot of curious gunmen today. One of them might recognize me. If so, they'll probably grab me in the morning.'

Reese explained a plan of action, with Jared and Wyatt also contributing. The war council lasted two hours. Then Brett and Shane returned via the long route to the wash. Shane patted Brett on the shoulder as a parting gesture.

'You're one of my heroes,' Shane said. 'Get yourself kilt and I'll drop you from the list.'

Brett grunted. 'Thanks for the words of encouragement. Don't let us down tomorrow night.'

'Me and Beauty will be there. Not to worry.'

Brett made his way back to Brimstone. It was after midnight by the time he scaled the rope and eased quietly into his room. He had barely gotten into bed when the door opened. A man was standing with a lantern in one hand and a gun in the other.

'The deception is over, my friend,' Montgomery spoke firmly. 'Let's take a walk.'

8

Desiree was asleep when the knock came at her door. She sat up as Lucia poked her head inside.

'I'm sorry, señorita, but I need for you to come with me,' she said anxiously.

'What's the matter?'

'Please,' she said softly. '*Por favor.*'

Desiree didn't bother to dress. Slipping on her robe, she followed Lucia down to Tynan's office.

Tynan and Montgomery were inside the room, along with Brett. He was fully dressed, but without his hat or gun. He had a shame-faced expression, ducking his head and not looking at her.

'Miss Desiree,' Tynan began an apology. 'I'm so sorry to have awakened you at this hour.'

'What's this about?'

'It's your bodyguard here. One of the men recognized him as a U.S. Marshal,'

Tynan announced. 'Being a bandit stronghold, you understand why we can't tolerate a lawman in town.'

'Two fellows robbed a train some time back. A detective tried to come in here and arrest them, but he was beaten nearly to death and sent on his way. I wanted to find out if they were still here. I had never seen them in person so I thought it would be safe.'

'Turns out, it wasn't those bandits who knew you,' Tynan told him. 'It was a delivery driver who happened to bring a load of produce and food from one of our suppliers. He was on the street when you went to the rescue of that little girl. He had previously seen you arrest a man over in Durango during a freight delivery.'

Brett shook his head. 'A town full of wanted men and a law-abiding citizen exposes me.'

Before anyone could speak, the door to the office was thrown open. A wild-eyed young man frantically waved his arms. 'I . . . ' He swallowed to get breath into his lungs. 'I couldn't stop him, Mr Tynan! Your brother, he broke into the prisoner's room!'

Montgomery and Brett both reacted at once, racing out of the door. They bolted down the hallway to Scarlet's room. The enforcer threw open the door to find Scarlet struggling with Dillon, slapping, clawing and kicking. That all came to an abrupt halt.

Montgomery grabbed Dillon's shoulders and pulled him away from the lady. As Dillon was spun around, Brett met him with a powerful smash to his jaw. Before the man knew he'd been hit, a second punch drove him down to all fours.

'I got this!' Montgomery growled at Brett, jumping between him and Dillon. 'Back off.'

Brett raised his hands to shoulder height, displaying his cooperation, then retreated out of the room. Scarlet didn't have time to react. Lucia was immediately at her side, looking over her superficial injuries. A puffy lip and red welt on her cheek showed where Dillon had hit her.

'That animal came in here demanding I submit to him!' Scarlet snapped at Tynan, who had arrived last. 'You promised that he would leave me alone!'

'I had a guard posted,' Tynan replied weakly. 'It isn't my fault if the man was too much of a coward to stand up to Dillon. This won't happen again.'

Scarlet's chest was still rising and falling rapidly from her strenuous fight. She took a moment to look at Brett and Montgomery. 'Thank you — both of you,' she conveyed her gratitude. 'I would not have been able to fight him off much longer.'

Brett nodded. 'I'm only sorry we were so long in getting here, ma'am.'

'I want Landau up here at nights from now on,' Tynan ordered.

Montgomery replied, 'I'll get him, boss. Dillon won't try anything with him keeping watch.'

The impotent guard helped Dillon to

his feet and half-carried him from the room. Lucia remained with Scarlet, while Desiree was bid goodnight. Tynan ordered Brett to accompany him and the enforcer escorted Brett down the hallway and out of the Snake Pit. He was led to a solid-looking building behind the general store. From the lingering aroma, Brett figured it to be a smokehouse for curing meat.

'You'll spend the rest of the night here,' Tynan informed him. 'Tomorrow, we'll decide what is to be done with you.'

'I didn't intend any trouble,' Brett maintained. 'I was searching for those two bandits.'

Tynan ignored his excuse and suggested, 'The lady upstairs seemed to know you.'

'Oh? Who was she?'

'I saw your rage at my brother's actions, and you never did say what your last name is.'

'Ask the teamster with the big mouth. He's the one who seems to know everything.'

'I think,' Tynan said, 'you are either a Valeron, or you're working with their family.'

Brett kept a poker expression. 'Valeron? You telling me that female prisoner you're holding upstairs is a Valeron?' Then he initiated a mock laughter. 'You must be in one big hurry to die. That family will burn this town to the ground and kill every single man in the process.'

'Word is,' Montgomery interjected, 'that one of the Valeron clan is a U.S. Marshal.'

Brett lifted a careless shoulder. 'You best not worry about me, fella. Worry about the dire mess you've gotten yourself into. Give it some thought — we can discuss your limited options.'

'What makes you think I won't hang you?' Tynan threatened.

'Do that a lot, do you?' Brett challenged. 'Hang every lawman that shows up?'

'You could be the exception to the rule.'

'Think before you act, Dwyer,' Brett

warned him. 'Sit down with me tomorrow and we can maybe discuss a way out of this fix that will save your town and your life.'

Tynan backed up so Montgomery could shut the door. As a bolt was set in place, one of them whispered, 'Sleep well, Mr Marshal.'

★   ★   ★

Desiree wasted no time the next morning. She marched down the hall to Tynan's office and tapped lightly at the door. Entering when invited, Tynan didn't look like he'd gotten much sleep. Red, tired eyes were housed by a shadowed pair of dark sockets. He had been concentrating so hard that two furrowed lines were severely etched into his forehead.

'Yes, Miss Moore. What is it?'

'I want to know what you are going to do with my bodyguard,' she said brusquely. 'I don't feel safe leaving my room without an escort.'

'Denim has offered to accompany

183

you to Cookie's Hash House and will be available whenever you need him.'

'And what about tomorrow? I can't make the journey to Santa Fe without Brett.'

'You expect me to turn him loose?'

'Yes.' She was decisive. 'You can't very well keep a U.S. Marshal penned up, and you would be the biggest fool this side of your brother if you were to harm him in any way.'

'If it's an escort to Santa Fe that worries you, Denim can take you.'

Desiree folded her arms in defiance. 'Mr Tynan, I came here to entertain. Brett is the best bodyguard I've ever had. I'm sure I can convince him to not make any trouble for you or those two robbers he was looking for.'

'I'm not so sure he came here for any bandits. I think he's looking for his sister.'

Desiree demonstrated consternation. 'His sister!' she gasped. 'You don't mean that woman down the hall from me . . . the prisoner?'

Tynan swallowed a lump — probably tasted like stupidity going down — as he realized he had dug himself a second hole! 'Look what you've done, young lady!' he said heavily. 'I've gone and told you about our captive — a woman whose presence is going to ruin my life.'

'What do you mean?'

Tynan expelled a deep breath. 'Dillon pulled the dumbest stunt of his life — and that's saying something for him,' he admitted. 'He kidnapped a girl he took a fancy to. In the midst of the confusion and tussle during the abduction, one of the men with him killed her fiancé.'

'My goodness! That's terrible!'

'It gets worse,' Tynan confessed. 'The young lady turned out to be a Valeron.'

Desiree remained openly aghast at his confession. 'Valeron! Not the Valerons who own that massive ranch on the Colorado-Wyoming border!'

'Yes. And I'm betting your escort's last name is Valeron, and kin to the lady down the hall. If I let him go, he'll return with enough men to destroy this town and kill everyone in it.'

Desiree soberly turned her head from side to side. 'I wouldn't want to be you,' she murmured.

'I'm not a killer or kidnapper, Miss Moore!' he declared. 'I formed a gang a good many years ago, but we only robbed Wells-Fargo, or companies like the railroad or freight outfits that were making plenty of money. The robberies were well planned so that no one got hurt — not even the companies. After all, most of them were financially well off enough to ensure the safety of other people's money.

'When I found Lucia, living the life of a slave, I purchased her for a companion. It took some time, but Lucia and I grew to love each other, deeply. That's when I decided to build this town. It was a sanctuary for outlaws, one where I charged each outlaw a few dollars a week to keep them safe. It meant hiring men that weren't as ethical as me, but it's been a safe haven since it was built. After a time, men and women — even a few families with kids — came here to discard their criminal lives or escape their poverty. They now work for me and I pay them well. This has become more than a bandit stronghold, it is a town of second chances.'

'And you stand to lose everything because of your brother's single act.'

Tynan groaned. 'There must be something I can do to get out of this confounded mess.'

Desiree stepped over next to the desk and formed a hopeful countenance. 'Perhaps there is.' At his curious upward glance, she went on. 'Have you spoken to Brett?'

'What good would that do?' he queried. 'Dillon and the others are responsible for the death of the kidnapped lady's betrothed. The Valeron clan are going to want their pound of flesh.'

'I doubt they want to destroy a whole town to get the guilty few.'

'Maybe not,' Tynan said. 'But he's going to want Dillon and the others. How can I sit by and let my own brother be taken away in chains?'

'The least you can do is talk to Brett. If you're right and he came for his kin, he must have a plan in place. He's the one you need to talk to.'

'Denim is waiting at the foot of the stairs for you. Why don't you go have breakfast and let me think about this for a bit? When you return, maybe we'll go see the marshal together.'

'All right.' Desiree reached for the door as it suddenly opened. Lucia had a tray with two plates of food and coffee. She hesitated until Desiree held the door open so she could enter. They each said a good morning and Desiree went out to the hallway and closed the door behind her. She listened a moment before stepping away.

'Ah, my love,' Tynan spoke softly. 'Just what I needed — breakfast and your counsel.'

'Anything you want, dear,' Lucia cooed her reply. 'You know that.'

This might be a bandit stronghold, Desiree thought, but I don't want to see any harm come to those two!

*   *   *

A few minutes after Desiree had left, Dillon pushed open Tynan's door and entered the office. The bruises on his face stood out, but his tightly slanted eyes and grim set of his jaw were enough to warn of impending trouble.

'Damn it all, Ty!' his brother wailed. 'I brought that woman hundreds of miles to be my bride. I ain't gonna wait no longer!'

'You agreed to be patient.'

'I've been patient! And it ain't worked! It's killing me — tearing at my guts. I can't sleep or eat.'

'For the love of . . . ' Tynan didn't finish the expression, but his face contorted into a controlled rage. 'Dillon, for once in your life, act like a grown man!'

'Who's in the smokehouse?' Dillon switched subjects. 'Kitchard wouldn't tell me.'

'I had the singer's bodyguard thrown in there for attacking you.' Tynan shrugged. 'Can't have someone busting my brother's puss, not when Denim was there to break up the scuffle between you and our captive. I didn't want you trying to sneak in there and get even.'

Dillon laughed. 'You don't think I'm that stupid?'

'I've always given you a certain amount of credit,' Tynan muttered.

Uncertain if that was a compliment or insult, Dillon stated, 'Brett is a tough customer. I've never been hit as hard as those two shots to my jaw.'

'Denim will let him out in a little while,' Tynan said. 'When he does, I'll have a talk with him and lay out a few rules. He won't be a problem again.'

'Yeah, he didn't have to knock my teeth loose. I wouldn't have hurt the girl.'

'You hit her in the face,' Tynan reminded him.

'Did I?' Dillon scowled. 'Don't remember that. Must have been my instinct for survival — 'cause of her kicking, clawing and biting me.'

'Think about how hard she fought.

190

Are you willing to kill her to get what you want?'

Dillon sneered. 'What's mine is mine. If she wants a fight, I'll give her one.'

'You promised me a week,' Tynan reiterated. 'I expect you to honor our agreement.'

'Yeah, OK,' Dillon grumbled. Then with a sneer of defiance, 'But then I'm taking her — whether you like it or not!'

Tynan didn't argue. 'Who's on guard tonight?'

'I did like you asked. Sike and Ricky will be at the west end, with Elmo and Kitchard at the other. The boys think you're picking on them for kidnapping a bride.' He frowned. 'Landau ought to be the fourth guard, instead of Kitchard.'

'Landau is going to watch Scarlet until the week is up. If he'd have been upstairs last night, he could have saved you getting your teeth rattled.'

'Yeah, yeah, I know. Landau don't cotton to any rough stuff with a woman.'

'What about Waco?'

'Waco is going to keep an eye here in

town on anyone coming or going.'

'Good. I don't want any mistakes. We can't take a chance on any of the Valerons showing up.'

'Stop worrying, Ty. The Valerons won't never find the girl, not in a thousand years.'

★   ★   ★

By asking Montgomery a couple of questions about housing, Desiree learned the two bandits were staying at one of the three 'bunkhouse' buildings. She also discovered how he had become the town enforcer, having killed a crooked sheriff and his deputy at a border town. He didn't support the kidnapping of a woman by Dillon, but he knew Tynan was a fair-minded man. He followed his orders, though not without questioning his decision on occasion.

After her meal, with Montgomery having a cup of coffee to keep her company, they returned to the upstairs office. Tynan was ready and waiting. He picked up his hat and gave Montgomery a nod. I'll take care of the lady from here, Denim. Keep an eye on Dillon and see he doesn't get into trouble.'

'Full-time job, watching that brother of yours.'

Tynan didn't reply, but took Desiree's arm in a gentlemanly fashion and escorted her to the smokehouse. She recognized the guard as one who often accompanied Montgomery.

'Kitchard,' Tynan addressed him, 'prisoner been fed?'

'Yes, sir. A couple hours ago.'

'You can go get some rest. I know you're pulling night guard duty.' Kitchard thanked him and left. Tynan didn't hesitate but opened the door to the shed.

Brett looked refreshed, as if he'd gotten a good night's sleep. He didn't attempt to exit the building until the boss of Brimstone gestured him out.

'You said we should talk,' Tynan began. 'I'm listening.'

'How'd you like to take a ride?' Brett

asked. 'I've got something you ought to see.'

'Right. I ride out of town so you can take me prisoner and trade for Scarlet?'

'No, I want to show you how to save your life, the life of Lucia, and the lives of everyone else in town.'

Tynan might have laughed at the absurdity of his claim, but Brett was not smiling.

'You really should go with Brett,' Desiree urged. 'He is an honorable man.'

'I can't stand by and let you hang my brother,' Tynan vowed.

'Then you and everyone in this town will perish,' Brett told him gravely. 'Let me show you what you're up against . . . then make your decision.'

'Where is it you want me to go?'

'Just a short way out of town, a half mile beyond where you are patrolling. I give you my word that both of us will return, and I will remain your prisoner, should you so demand.'

'All right, I'll take a chance you are telling the truth. And,' he put a cool glare on him, 'Miss Moore will stay here as collateral. If something happens to me . . . '

'The only thing that will happen to you is seeing the futility of going to war with my family.'

Tynan was desperate enough to take a chance. 'Let's escort Miss Moore back to her room.'

Denim Montgomery was near the front of the Snake Pit. He hurried over to meet the three of them, curious as to what was going on.

'See Miss Moore upstairs. Tell Lucia to provide her with whatever she needs.'

'You turning the marshal loose?'

'Keep his identity to yourself,' Tynan ordered. 'We're going to take a short ride and discuss a few things. We should be back in an hour or so.'

The enforcer did not hide his confusion, but didn't question the orders. 'Whatever you say, boss.' Then he stepped forward to stand at Desiree's side. She extended an arm for him to take and they entered the Snake Pit together.

Lucia opened the door as Landau pushed the portable bathing tub into Scarlet's room. It was more than half-full of steaming hot water. He didn't say a word, yet did glance over at her. She was struck immobile by the look. It was enigmatic and complex. She wondered if he had developed feelings for her, or was he conflicted because he objected to keeping a woman against her will?

'Thank you, Mr Landau,' she said, fixing her gaze on him.

'It's Queen,' he replied softly. 'Landau is my first name, after my mother's side of the family.'

There it was, a minute's break in the man's taciturn character. He had told her of his private life, something personal he hadn't shared with anyone else. Now she had a name.

'Thank you, Mr Queen,' Scarlet corrected, allowing a gentleness to her voice.

He didn't speak again, but left the room at once. Lucia stared after him and then turned her attention to Scarlet.

'You know,' she said, marveled, 'I never knew Landau had a last name. It's the first I've heard of it, and he's been with us almost two years.'

'I'm amazed that you can provide such a luxury out here in the middle of a desert,' Scarlet put her attention on the expensive tub.

The woman smiled — more a friendly simper than that of a captor to a prisoner. 'It's one of my extravagant pleasures. Tynan bought the tub and the heating tank system in San Francisco. It was shipped here and a water line was hooked up from the one bringing drinking water to our town.' She laughed. 'Tynan is such a dear. He does everything he can to see to my comfort.'

'It's a shame he has such a ruthless brother, one who will destroy all you've built.'

The warmth left Lucia's face, but she did not defend Dillon. 'I had the dress freshly cleaned and pressed. I will bring it up, once you've had time to bathe and wash your hair. Do you need anything else? Another brush, a ribbon or pins to hold your hair in place?'

Scarlet gave a negative gesture and Lucia said, 'The entertainer will be on stage a short while after supper.'

'It's very thoughtful of you and Tynan to let me attend the show.'

Lucia hesitated at the doorway. 'At the trial — you know the man who is escorting the singer, don't you?'

Scarlet maintained a supine expression. 'Do I?'

'Tynan has discovered he is a U.S. Marshal. He believes he is a Valeron.'

'There are a lot of Valerons,' Scarlet dismissed the information. 'I couldn't see the man very clearly because of the veil you forced me to wear.'

'We have a hundred gunmen in this town. I don't see any way your family can get you out without it costing many lives on both sides.'

'I told you earlier, if I were to escape,

then there would be no fight and no killing.'

'Tynan is worried about what Dillon would do.'

'Let me worry about Dillon. If he comes after me, it will be the last thing he ever does.'

'Because your family is close by?'

Scarlet didn't answer.

After a moment, Lucia took a step back. 'I'll give you an hour or so before I remove the bath. Supper will be at the usual time.'

'Thank you for your kindness, Lucia. I do not hold you responsible for my captivity.'

9

Brett and Tynan returned after a couple of hours. Tynan spoke to Montgomery and went into the Snake Pit alone. Brett took care of the two horses and arrived to take Desiree to lunch at the normal time.

'What happened?' Desiree was frantic. 'I've been having terrible thoughts of being forced to watch you be hanged, like those two who caused the nun's death!'

'Everything is going as planned,' he said, imbuing his words with confidence. 'Let's get a table in a corner so we can discuss your show tonight.'

'My show?'

Brett escorted her across the street to Cookie's Hash House. Once they were seated at a secluded table and had ordered their meal, he began to explain.

'Wait a minute!' Desiree interrupted.

'You aren't kidding? You have an opening act before I sing tonight?'

'That's right. I need the distraction so I can complete my assignment.'

'I thought the assignment was to get Scarlet out alive?'

Brett's expression hardened. 'Fred Logan was killed while defending the woman he was going to marry; his parents were beaten unconscious; and Dillon kidnapped Scarlet with the intent of making her his personal slave for the rest of her life. My family can't let those crimes go unpunished.'

The girl was stunned. 'You can't mean you intend to arrest all of the men involved?'

'Probably not Landau. Tynan claimed he has been very protective of Scarlet and only tended to the horses during the attack. I'm not even aware of any warrant being out for his arrest.'

'Even so, there are five men you will have to — '

'Seven,' he corrected. 'We're going to take the two you came after, too.'

Desiree could not prevent a cynical laugh. She covered her mouth quickly, fearful a hysterical outbreak would draw the attention of everyone in the place. 'Brett!' she gasped, recovering her aplomb. 'Had I known you were crazy, I wouldn't have agreed to come with you!'

'Agreed?' Brett countered. 'I recall you forced your way into making this trip.'

'Yes, but that's when I thought you were an intelligent man, a man of character . . . and quite charming. I had no idea you were hiding a suicidal tendency beneath your cool veneer.'

'Veneer?' He displayed puzzlement. 'I have veneer?' Then he shook his head. 'Wonder if that's something my brother Nash can cure?'

'Very funny!' she retorted, without a trace of humor.

The food arrived and the young fellow gave Desiree extra milk and sugar, before asking if he could get her anything else. She thanked him and rewarded his efforts with a comely smile. The warm look on her face vanished as soon as the kid left.

'Brett, tell me you aren't going to get a lot of people killed! Some of the townsfolk are as innocent as that boy. I've seen a few children, and the people running these establishments hired on because they were down on their luck. They aren't criminals.'

'Dad-gum!' Brett complained. 'When a man allows a gal to kiss him, he kind of expects that she has a little faith in him.'

'You *allowed* . . . ' she sputtered. 'You kissed me first!'

'Because I have faith in you. I trust you to do whatever is necessary to complete our mission.'

'I'm doing my part,' she argued. 'I will sing my heart out tonight!'

'And I'll take care of the rest.'

'At the price of how many bodies?'

Brett took a bite of food before answering. He swallowed, then gave Desiree a wholly sincere look. 'A few men might die tonight. Sometimes that can't be helped. But our plan is to get in, get the job done, and get out, without any killing whatsoever.'

'That sounds utterly impossible!'

'Yes, my lovely songbird,' he replied smugly. 'And that's why it will work.'

★ ★ ★

Tynan glanced up from his desk when Montgomery entered and asked at once, 'What's Dillon up to?'

'He's been spending most of his time with Waco over at the Red Hare. He's been talking again, gaining support. I think he intends to take over as boss of Brimstone.'

'Yes, his lust for the Valeron girl has increased his ambition to run this town.'

'Want me to start gathering men to support us?'

'No,' Tynan said. 'I'm thinking of retiring to the position of mayor or something. The days of this being a bandit stronghold are coming to an end. You'll likely end up as town marshal.'

Montgomery laughed. 'Guess I can stop worrying. What about tonight?'

'Scarlet will watch the show with us.

She will wear a veil to hide her face.'

'What about Brett?'

'He's leaving in the morning. The two of us reached an understanding.'

As was his habit, Montgomery didn't question the decision. He waited patiently until Tynan turned to why he had summoned him.

'There is going to be a second entertainer tonight. I want you to spread the word and have as many men attend as possible.'

The enforcer grinned. 'Don't tell me Brett is going to play the guitar and sing, too?'

'Actually, it's a rather unusual act.' He grunted. 'I offered to have you lend a hand. The kid performing needs someone to do a couple chores during his act. I don't trust anyone else to be backstage with Miss Moore.'

'She's something special,' Montgomery acknowledged.

'I've been assured it's nothing difficult or that anyone will make fun about later.'

'Sure, I'll be glad to help out.'

'And pass the word there will be free drinks at the end of the show. Invite Dillon to come. Perhaps a show and free drinks will improve his mood.'

'Nothing but getting his hands on that gal down the hall will do that, boss. He's serious about taking over . . . '

'That's mostly hard liquor talking.'

'I don't know,' Montgomery warned. 'Even before the raid into Colorado, Dillon was complaining that you were getting soft. There comes a time when a younger wolf stops following the leader of the pack. He begins to think he ought to be the top dog.'

Rather than refute his concern, Tynan waved him off. 'Let everyone in town know about the additional entertainer tonight. Show will start the same time as usual.'

'I'll spread the word,' the enforcer assured him. Then he left the room.

Tynan thought about his brother. He knew the younger man no longer respected his authority. Dillon considered him as too soft with age and the sharing of his life with Lucia. He would contest his authority one day soon. Worst of all, the feud would come about because of a woman. He had grabbed a proper lady, turned her life to shambles, yet expected her to respond to him like a lamb alone in the wilderness.

Tynan leaned back and closed his eyes. He was the founder of Brimstone. It was up to him to make decisions that were the best for everyone in town. With the law moving into the south west, there would soon be no room for an outlaw stronghold. That meant turning Brimstone into an honest-to-goodness settlement. And while they would continue to allow wanted men to visit or stay with impunity, the streets would be safe so as to encourage settlers to start ranches or farms nearby. It was progress and a necessity. Logically and practically, his brother did not fit in a civilized world.

★　★　★

The fun started when the curtain opened. It took a moment before the crowd took notice of Shane standing well off to one side. Oddly, he was wearing a wide-brim sombrero and had another in each hand. A uniquely colored horse became visible, moving up behind him. Lowering its head, the animal pushed against his back until he took an involuntary step forward.

A number of men began to laugh and a couple yelled encouragement. The horse repeated the push, forcing Shane out to the center of the stage. There he stopped and turned to face the horse.

'All right!' he said loudly. 'I'm here! So quit pushing.'

The horse moved her head up and down, as if satisfied.

'Gentlemen . . . and ladies.' Shane rotated back around to speak to the audience. 'This impetuous animal here is Beauty, the smartest horse in the . . . ' He paused as if considering his words and finished with 'room!'

Some laughter.

'While I demonstrate Beauty's intelligence,' Shane continued, 'I have to keep an eye on her.' As he spoke, he turned slowly to one side. The horse suddenly grabbed the rim of his sombrero between her teeth and gave her head a toss. The hat sailed well back into the gathering.

'Dag-nab it,' Shane cried out. 'I knew I couldn't trust you!'

More laughter.

'What'd I tell you? This is not only a smart horse, but she's sneaky fast.' He took a moment to don the second hat. Then he rotated about and gave Beauty a wide grin. 'See? I came prepared for your mischief.' Pivoting back to the audience, he began again. 'It won't do you any good to steal my . . . '

Beauty snatched the hat and tossed her head, flinging the second sombrero into the crowd.

Shane spun on her. 'Oh yeah?' he shouted. 'You think you can get the best of me, do you?'

Beauty's head bobbed up and down.

'Well, I brought a third hat,' Shane announced, placing the last hat on his head. 'And this time I won't make the mistake of turning my back on you. In fact, I'll stand alongside of you so you can't . . . '

But as Shane moved, his head was turned enough that Beauty repeated the theft of his hat, sending the third sombrero flying out to the spectators. Shane spun about and pointed a finger at Beauty. 'Was that you?' he demanded to know. 'Did you just steal my last hat?'

Beauty stared straight forward and moved her head from side to side.

'Don't lie to me!' Shane barked. 'I know it was you.'

With his finger still pointed at Beauty, she again gave her head a somewhat negative shake.

'Mister?' Denim Montgomery moved out on the stage. 'Are you about ready to do a trick?'

'Yeah, yeah,' Shane laced his voice with bitterness. 'Bring out the buckets.'

The enforcer hurried to put a bucket

behind both Beauty's left and right rear hoofs. Then he returned to grab an empty beer keg. He brought it forward, but stood off to one side, not aligned behind the animal.

'All right,' Shane spoke up for the crowd to hear. 'Beauty, show how smart you are.' He pointed at a woman in the front. 'Tell Beauty which bucket to kick, the one on her left or her right.'

'Left!' she complied.

Beauty struck out with her left back foot and the first bucket went rolling across the stage.

'Now right!' Shane commanded.

Again, Beauty kicked the bucket, but with her right rear foot.

Denim placed the barrel behind Beauty and retrieved the buckets. Shane turned his body so he could mostly face the horse. 'Now both feet!' he ordered.

Beauty bucked forward so she could kick the barrel. It flew ten feet before it hit the stage floor. Before the applause died out, Shane again had everyone's attention.

'Now, to prove how smart she is. Beauty,' he asked the horse, 'how many times did you kick?'

Beauty pawed the wooden platform three times. Shane gave her a pat on the head and looked out at the audience.

'You folks are probably thinking I taught the horse to count to three, so how about a random number? Someone . . . ' He pointed at a man near the front. 'Give me a number between one and six.' He quickly added, 'Beauty gets bored when she has to pound out a large number. As I'm out of hats, she would likely throw me off the stage if you chose a hundred.'

'Five!' the man shouted.

Shane faced the horse. 'Five is the number, Beauty. Count to five.'

And, as Shane counted with her, Beauty pawed the stage exactly five times.

There was a round of applause. Then Shane spoke to Beauty again. 'I think we've about used up our time. Where's the lovely Desiree with the beautiful voice?'

Beauty backed up a step or two, turned

around and went toward the curtain. When she reached the spot, Desiree moved into sight. Beauty maneuvered in behind her and began nudging her out on the stage until she was next to Shane.

'What an amazing animal!' Desiree exclaimed.

'She ain't so smart,' Shane said. 'I beat her three games out of five at checkers just yesterday!'

Desiree patted the horse just behind her ear. 'I think you're a very smart horse.'

Beauty stretched out her right leg, tucked her left under her, and lowered her head in a bow.

More applause and cheering.

'How about me?' Shane cried out. 'What did you think of my performance?'

Desiree waited until Beauty was standing again. At Shane's question, she tickled the underside of Beauty's chin. The horse rolled her upper lip upward and pumped her head up and down while uttering a jeering whinny.

'I guess you get the horse laugh,' Desiree teased.

'You'd best remember the other tricks my horse can do,' Shane warned. 'After all, I'm out of hats, but that dress you're wearing is mighty tempting. If you were to turn your back on Beauty, she might decide to send your skirt flying.'

Desiree immediately sidestepped away from Beauty. It brought more mirth and a few off-color comments about ladies' unmentionables. The singer ignored the catcalls and extended a hand toward both Shane and the horse.

'How about a nice hand for our special act tonight?'

Shane moved alongside Beauty and had her bow once more, and they were showered with boisterous hand-clapping and some cheers. Then he and the horse left the stage to disappear behind the side curtain.

Desiree signaled to Piano Man. He pounded out an introductory musical strain, and she began to sing 'Sweet Genevieve'. The crowd settled down to enjoy Desiree's wonderful singing voice.

Brett hired the boy and his parents from Cookie's Hash House to cater the free drinks. After all, they didn't have any business while the show was in progress anyway. He had gotten twelve bottles of whiskey from the bartender and placed them in a box. Once Shane took the stage, the bartender moved to the far end of the bar, seeking a better vantage spot from which to watch the show. Brett discreetly picked up the case of booze and took it into the store room.

Quickly, he prepared each bottle of alcohol for the giveaway at the end of the show. Five minutes later, Brett stepped back out and returned the dozen bottles to their original location. He completed his task with no time to spare. Shane was weaving through the audience, leaving the saloon with Beauty, taking her to the livery.

Thinking of a thousand things that might go wrong, Brett glimpsed up at the balcony and saw his sister was there, once more with her face hidden by a veil. Along with her were three others — Tynan, Lucia and Landau.

He didn't allow his gaze to linger. The time was too near to risk anyone taking notice. This was it. Even as Desiree lifted her next number to the rafters, he was busy surveying the crowd. It was worrisome not finding Waco or Dillon among them. That could mean trouble later on.

Shane returned after putting up the horse. 'Everything ready?' he asked, his face flushed with excitement. 'Do you think this will work?'

'Our three servers are just inside the bat-wing doors, the man, woman and teenage boy,' Brett pointed out. 'Give them two bottles each. Then grab a couple yourself. I'll have another bottle or two handy and the bartender will also help with the filling of glasses. Tell the servers not to give more than a half glass to anyone — we don't want to run out. Everyone is to wait for the toast.

Be careful not to miss anyone.'

'I got it. Everyone is to raise their glass together in salute after Desiree's last song.'

'That's the idea.'

Shane gathered up six bottles from the box and went to distribute them to the servers. Brett waited for him to come back and worried about handling those who weren't in attendance. There were quite a few men missing besides Dillon and Waco, gunmen who might cause trouble.

Shane returned to join him and reported the three waiters were prepared to start serving.

'Desiree will end with 'Jeanie with the Light Brown Hair'. Soon as she starts, we move.'

'Scarlet is on the balcony,' Shane whispered. 'Does she know we are coming for her tonight?'

'She's smart enough to know that you being here with that trick horse means something. She will be ready.' He grinned at Shane. 'Good thing you brought along that carnival horse.'

'Performed like she was still on tour,' Shane agreed. 'Even took her cue from the girl.'

'Desiree has more courage than any woman I ever met.'

Shane stood silent for a few moments. Brett waited, knowing he had a question. His voice was somewhat trepid when he finally spoke.

'You think we'll have to shoot our way out of town tonight?'

'It may come to that,' Brett gave an honest evaluation. 'We have a plan, but that doesn't mean there won't be trouble. Your first job is to get Scarlet out safely. Did you ready getaway horses for the three of us, just in case?'

'It was easy. I seen the hostler down in the front row when me and Beauty were on stage. There was no one around at the livery.'

'Yes, things worked out here, too. The bartender had to move to the bar counter to watch your act. It gave me the time and privacy I needed.'

'What'd you think about me on stage?'

Brett displayed reservations. 'To be painfully honest, you best keep working on the ranch. I'm afraid you'd starve on your own with any kind of road show.'

'You heard the audience laugh!'

'Have to wonder if that's because you were good, or because you were so bad?'

Shane snorted his contempt. 'Now I know why Uncle Locke never asked you to come back to help manage the ranch. You've got no eye for talent.'

Brett laughed. 'All right, little cousin. I admit you were almost as good as the horse. Not any better, mind you, but almost as good.'

'What about Desiree? If things go badly, she might end up locked in a room next to Scarlet!'

'Regardless of what happens, Tynan promised to let her leave tomorrow without any trouble.'

Shane didn't have time for more questions. Desiree announced that this was her last song. It was the signal for them to get started.

★   ★   ★

Cliff rode hard and stopped in a cloud of dust. The two guards had come riding from out of the darkness to block his path.

'Did you see her?' Cliff cried. 'The little orphan girl! She disappeared while I was watering my horse. I've been searching for hours.'

Sike and Ricky had both seen Cliff when he was in town earlier. Sike grunted. 'You mean the squirt run off on you?'

'I've got to find her!'

Ricky shook his head. 'Look, mister, it ain't our business to watch for . . . '

'Keep your hands away from your guns!' a voice commanded.

Out of the blackness of the night, Jared and Reese came forward with their guns drawn.

'What the hey?' Ricky mumbled.

'Sit your bronc easy!' Reese snarled the words. 'Unbuckle your gun-belts and let them drop. Then climb down from your horses.'

The two men did as they were told. Jared and Reese bound them quickly with buckskin straps and proceeded to drape them over their horses on their stomachs. With a piece of rope each, they secured the men's wrists to their ankles under the horse's belly.

'There you go,' Reese announced to Cliff when they had finished. 'Take them to the meeting place. Soon as Wyatt and the boys do their job, you'll have another couple to look after.'

'These two were in on the kidnapping and murder,' Jared said, crystals of ice on every word. 'Hanging is too good for them!'

'All in good time, little brother,' Reese told him. 'Brett is a law-abiding marshal. We do things his way.'

Cliff added, 'Nessy and I will keep watch on them, Jared. You've still got a job to do.'

'OK,' Jared acquiesced. 'But I still think it'd be smarter to kill 'um as we catch 'um.'

'Let's head for town,' Reese said. 'Brett and Scarlet are counting on us.'

'Good luck!' Cliff called to them. Then he took up the reins of the two horses and started off for the waiting area.

Meanwhile, at the other end of town, Wyatt and the two ranch hands had captured the other two guards. The two of them had been sitting on a rock and sharing a bottle. They were half-drunk and none too happy about being bound up and tossed over the backs of their horses. Reb took charge of them and started off toward the meeting place.

10

After serving the drinks, Shane slipped out of the saloon and was waiting at the edge of town. It took a few minutes, but Reese, Dodge, Jared and Wyatt arrived to meet him.

'How'd it go?' Wyatt was the one to ask.

'It's a good thing we're meeting here. I saw a couple men watching the street. You'd have been spotted in a second if you had entered town from that direction.'

'Any idea where Dillon or Waco is at?'

'No, and Brett thinks the two bandits we're after have joined with Dillon's bunch. He told me they didn't show up at the saloon tonight. Did you have any trouble with the sentries?'

Reese laughed. 'Not a bit. As Brett promised, three of the four were with

Dillon during his raid, so we don't have to look for them.'

'That will make it easier,' Jared agreed. 'Once we finish in town, I'll swing back and let the extra man go. We only want the kidnappers.'

'What now?' Shane asked. 'Brett is inside the Snake Pit saloon. He and the singer will need help to handle all of the men in there and manage to get Scarlet out of her room.'

'We better find out who is still on the prowl,' Reese outlined. 'Shane, you and Dodge slip along the north side of the street and check the second saloon for customers. Wyatt, Jared and me will take the south side. Meet us back at the Snake Pit. We don't want a war, so just advise people to stay off the streets. If they put up a fuss, you'll have to deal with them quietly.'

'Where are your horses?' Shane wanted to know.

'In the wash, maybe a hundred yards from here. If something goes wrong, we'll meet back there and possibly have to launch an all-out assault.'

'Sure hope that doesn't happen,' Shane said. 'Hate to wind up with dozens of people dead.'

'We do whatever is necessary to get Scarlet back unharmed,' Jared pledged.

Reese took control again. 'Let's not talk last resort until we see if our plan is going to work. Reb should be in position to cover our retreat by this time.'

'Keep things as quiet as possible,' Wyatt reminded everyone.

Jared gave an affirmative bob of his head. 'This is it,' he spoke the obvious. 'Scarlet is depending on us. Don't anyone make any mistakes.'

'Sounds like good advice,' Dodge interjected. 'Let's get to it.'

⋆　⋆　⋆

Brett watched the crowd anxiously, every nerve in his body on edge. A good many customers left the saloon after the show, but the chairs at the tables remained full. Piano Man was playing a laggard tune, as if he was feeling melancholy or reminded of a lullaby. The bartender had served the last of what remained of the free bottles of whiskey and was seated on a stool behind the bar. He had partaken of the toast and was relaxed, with his back against the wall, droopy eyed as he stared off into space.

'Good show tonight,' Montgomery said, wandering over to stand next to Brett. 'Seemed to have drained the energy of the whole crowd.'

'You did a good job on stage. Maybe you missed your true calling?'

'If you mean handling props for a horse act, I won't take it as a compliment.'

Brett laughed shortly, then spoke as if he had suddenly remembered something important. 'Oh, Tynan said he'd like to see you up in his office. I was supposed to tell you to visit right after the show. It kind of slipped my mind.'

Montgomery shrugged. 'I doubt it's

anything too important, but I'll sashay up thataway and see what he wants.'

Brett noticed the man's words were slurred and delivered in a slow and casual manner. The enforcer shut his eyes, then opened them wide. 'I must not have gotten enough sleep last night. I'm about two seconds away from dozing off.'

'Me, too,' Brett told him. 'I hope Desiree doesn't want an early start tomorrow.'

'I'm going to miss her. She really added some life to this dusty old burg.'

'She's something special, no doubt about it.'

Denim Montgomery jerked his head upward in farewell, then headed for the stairs, wobbling a little. It took him a long time to reach the balcony and hall, but he was soon out of sight.

A number of men were nodding off and several were sound asleep. A couple lay with their heads on the table, and two of the working ladies were sitting in one corner, shoulder-to-shoulder with their chins resting on their breast-bones, both snoozing. The muttering and conversations in the room were muffled and forced, as almost everyone still conscious was growing drowsy.

Desiree came down, having changed into a modest dress. Brett went to meet her and they moved together to stand next to the storeroom.

'Landau is still on guard duty,' she whispered. 'He didn't drink any of the whiskey. So long as he doesn't walk to the balcony, we won't have to worry about him until you go up to get Scarlet.'

'I don't expect him to object. He doesn't believe she should have ever been kidnapped.'

The young lady looked around, eyes broadened with the danger and excitement of the moment. She was game, but felt the same worry and uncertainty as Brett.

'Is this how it feels . . . when you expect to be shot and killed at any moment?'

'Nash providing us a bottle of chloral hydrate should save a lot of lives. By lacing those free drinks, almost every man who came to the show is unconscious.' Brett took a deep breath. 'Our main problem is not knowing where Dillon and Waco are at. They could cause us a lot of trouble.'

'How about my two road agents?'

'I haven't seen them, either, but Montgomery said they were hanging around with Dillon.'

'And the other men you're after?'

'Tynan arranged for three of them to be guarding the roads into town tonight. I warned Shane to keep an eye out for them.'

'So your family will have captured three of the kidnappers?'

'Should be awaiting transport to the nearest jailhouse by now. All we need to do is find the two you're after, along with Dillon and Waco. You should get a pat on the back and a nice little bonus for bringing those two in.'

'I owe it all to you.'

Brett enjoyed the way her eyes shone — so bright with enthusiasm . . . warm . . . beguiling. He was drawn forward, aching to feel her lips once more.

'Brett!' she stopped him breathlessly. 'Dillon's at the door!'

★ ★ ★

Four men, including Waco and Dillon, came storming into the Snake Pit together. Whatever their intentions, they stopped suddenly, agape at the bizarre scene. Being back by the store room, Brett and Desiree ducked out of sight.

'The two bandits are with Dillon!' the girl whispered.

'Dillon must be here to confront Tynan and take Scarlet by force,' Brett deduced.

'Landau won't allow him to touch her.'

'He can't take on four men!'

Dillon and the others looked around the room and saw nearly every man was asleep or incapacitated. 'What the hell?'

he roared. 'Hey! What's going on here?'

A mutter or two was uttered, with the loudest voice piping up to say, 'Quiet down!'

'They've been drugged!' Waco realized. 'Same as the couple we thought were drunk on the street. It was those free drinks. They were doctored to knock everyone out.'

Dillon pulled his gun and headed across the room. 'I'll let my brother know that we're taking over. You look around for that singer's bodyguard!'

Waco turned to the pair of gunmen at his side. 'Keep watch!' he commanded. 'The Valerons are behind this. Get to either side of the door and be ready.'

Brett could not let his kin walk into a trap, yet he couldn't risk running up the stairs after Dillon. He looked at Desiree. She only had her derringer and wouldn't be much help in a gunfight. Tynan had promised to allow the rescue to take place and Montgomery was likely passed out in his office. Landau would protect Scarlet, but he had to deal with Tynan's very determined brother.

Undecided as how to proceed, Brett caught a glimpse of Shane outside, only a few feet from the bat-wing doors. The decision was made. He pushed Desiree down behind a stack of boxes and stepped out from cover. Gun in hand, he shouted, 'Hold it, Waco! You're covered!'

Waco dropped to the floor, like someone had jerked a rug from under his feet. He quickly scrambled behind the bar for cover.

The two bandits both turned their guns on Brett. He had anticipated the reaction and fired off a single shot. It hit one of the pair in his gun-hand shoulder. He lost his weapon as Brett ducked down to avoid the bullets from the other man's gun.

Two slugs struck the door of the storeroom. Then, before another shot could be fired, Jared burst through the door and tackled the uninjured bandit. Shane, Reese and Wyatt also charged into the room. Dodge followed, but remained at the door to watch the street,

The struggle between Jared and the bandit lasted only two punches. Reese had his gun covering the wounded man and Wyatt announced, 'Fight's over!'

'I don't think so!' Dodge warned. 'We've got a bunch of men gathering in the street. They heard the shooting!'

'Take cover!' Brett shouted.

The five of them left the two bandits and scrambled towards Brett. They took cover behind a few boxes, overturned a faro table, and ducked behind the end of the bar counter. Waco was still at the other end. He crawled around the opposite end, hunched down with his gun.

'In here!' Waco shouted. 'It's a bunch of raiders, trying to grab the boss and his wife!'

A dozen men came boiling into the room, ready to fight.

* * *

Landau was on his feet, having heard the shots from downstairs. Dillon appeared at the end of the hallway and put his hand on his gun. 'Stay out of this, Landau.'

'You ain't going to touch the lady, Dillon!' Landau warned.

'She's mine! I found her!'

Landau started to walk forward. When Dillon attempted to draw his gun, he charged at him. Two long strides and he plunged into Dillon, catching hold of his arm, preventing him from getting the weapon free of its holster.

Dillon ceased trying to use the gun and the two men caromed off of the wall. They began to wrestle and struggle, each straining and grappling, trying to get the advantage over the other.

Landau was not as big as Dillon, but he had worked hard at times and was in better physical shape. His weakness was in not wanting to hurt Dillon. However, Dillon had made up his mind. He was not going to be put off by anyone. The commotion from downstairs went un-noticed by either man.

Dillon broke free and slugged Landau

alongside the head with his fist. He followed up with a roundhouse swing, but Landau ducked. Facing off against the larger man, Dillon's eyes were mere slits on his cheeks, his teeth clenched in rage, livid with his desire. He had come for Scarlet and would not be denied.

Blocking another punch that would have knocked him off his feet, Landau dug in and fought back. Dillon didn't wish to go toe-to-toe, knowing Landau was the better fighter. Stung by a right fist to the side of his face, Dillon snaked his gun free.

Landau grabbed his wrist and the two of them did a deadly dance in the hallway, slamming off one wall and bouncing off the other. When they reached Tynan's office, the door gave way. Lucia screamed and Tynan yelled at the pair to stop.

But Dillon would neither cease the battle nor relinquish the gun. He and Landau stumbled on past the doorway, out on to the balcony. Then he pulled the trigger. Landau felt a hot burning sensation along his ribs. It prompted him to double his efforts. Moving in closer, he planted his feet, and, with a mighty heave, jerked Dillon sideways, while attempting to yank the gun from his hand.

A second gunshot sounded, but it was muffled from having the muzzle tight against Dillon's chest. As Tynan came rushing out to the hallway, Dillon staggered backward and tumbled down the stairway. He rolled head-over-heels and landed in a twisted heap about half-way down.

Tynan continued out to the balcony. He glanced at Landau and then down at his brother. He saw the bunch of men who had gathered at the entrance, all primed and ready for a fight. Everyone in the place had stopped to watch the deadly match at the top of the stairs. He quickly raised a hand to prevent a violent gun battle on the casino floor.

'Stand easy, men!' he called down to the small army. 'The fighting is over.'

Landau went down to check on Dillon,

but the younger Dwyer's eyes were open and glazed in death. The bullet from his own gun had gone right through his heart. Landau lifted his head and offered reverently, 'I'm sorry, boss.'

Tynan gave him a consolatory nod and turned to address the men below.

'Brett, and you fellows, can lower your guns. Men,' he addressed the others, 'come in if you want.'

Several men flooded into the room and many sounded off with questions. After a moment, Tynan again took charge.

'There's no fight for any of you men,' Tynan assured them. 'This is a private matter.'

'What happened?' one piped up. 'How come everyone is — they ain't dead, are they?'

'None of them are dead,' Tynan answered. 'I made a choice to prevent the destruction of our town. Putting as many men to sleep as possible was part of the plan.'

'Destruction?' a fellow asked. 'From who?'

Reese was the one to answer. 'A half mile from here, one of our men is standing ready with a Gatling gun. Another man has a case of dynamite and can shoot an explosive-equipped arrow at a hundred yards and hit his target every time. Your boss has chosen to save the town and all of your lives. You'd best be thanking him.'

Tynan bobbed his head up and down. 'I saw the Gatling gun, boys. And those sticks of dynamite would level this town in a half dozen shots. We had no chance against the Valerons.'

'Valerons? Why're they here?' a confused gunman asked. 'What do they want?'

'We came to get back our kin,' Reese clarified. 'Dillon and his men kidnapped my sister and killed the man she was going to marry . . . on her wedding day.'

The news did not sit well with most of the men. Murder, robbery, cattle or horse rustling . . . that went with their profession. But stealing a bride-to-be and killing her would-be husband . . . on their wedding day no less. Hell, that was un-American.

Brett moved out slowly, gun ready to fire, searching for Waco. 'There's one kidnapper missing!' he announced loudly. 'Show yourself, Waco.'

The notorious gunman rose up slowly. His gun was out and he quickly pointed it at Desiree. Brett had not been aware that she was exposed. Now they were in a stand-off.

'Anyone tries taking my gun and I kill the songbird,' Waco warned.

Most of the men in the room grumbled their displeasure at his threat. However, it was Wyatt's voice that resounded within the room. He moved to stand a few feet from Brett. 'What kind of lowlife yellow snake threatens a woman?'

Waco gave him the once-over. 'You must be Wyatt Valeron.'

'That's me.' With a sneer of contempt, 'And I'll tell you, I never figured the Waco Kid was such a coward as to use a woman as a shield.'

Waco flicked a glance about and saw

he had no support from the men in the room. The news about Scarlet had turned the table on him and Dillon's other men. 'I don't like the odds,' he said, somewhat lamely.

Wyatt nodded to Brett and the others. 'Put your guns away. Waco can have his chance to walk.' He bore into him with a steady gaze. 'You can try your luck against me, Waco, or throw down your gun and take your chances with a judge and jury.'

Reese moved to where he could keep an eye on the wounded bandit and Jared eyed the other, transmitting a silent warning. Shane and Dodge both had hands on their guns but had not pulled their weapons. Brett looked at Wyatt long enough to glimpse his confident wink, then holstered his gun.

'There you are, Waco,' Wyatt said. 'It's me and you. Either drop the gun or step out in the clear and face me. If you take me, you can ride away.'

Waco studied Wyatt for a few endless seconds. He had heard the stories, knew Wyatt was supposed to be one of the fastest men alive. There was no doubt in his own mind that he had once been equal to or better than Wyatt, but he had not practised much since coming to Brimstone. His reputation kept men from crossing him. Now, with his very life on the line, he had to wonder if he was as good as his opponent, standing a mere twenty feet away.

'What'll it be, Waco?' Wyatt taunted him. 'Are you a man, or have you become a desert rat, hiding in a burrow or behind the skirts of a woman?'

Waco grit his teeth in a sneer. 'All right, Valeron.' The gun slid gently into its holster and he stepped out from behind the counter. 'I'm callin' your hand. Let's see just how fast you are.'

'Desiree,' Wyatt spoke to the girl without looking at her. 'Pick up a glass from the bar and hold it out in front of you. Stand off to the side far enough that neither of us can see you.'

The young lady did as he asked.

'Waco, when the glass hits the floor,

we draw. Fair enough?'

The gunman bent slightly into a crouch, his hand inches from the butt of his gun. 'Fair enough,' he grated in an unwavering, ice cold voice.

Wyatt took a deep breath and directed, 'All right, Desiree, drop the glass whenever you like.'

It took several seconds for the Pinkerton agent to find her courage. She knew the glass breaking would be the death of one man . . . perhaps both. She hesitated . . . then let it drop.

The sound of the glass impacting upon the floor was negligible, drowned out instantly by Wyatt's gun-blasts. He fired twice, making sure Waco had no chance to get a shot of his own. Then the room was silent, except for the sound of Waco, as he slumped lifelessly to the floor. He landed face down, with his gun lying next to his hand, unfired.

No one spoke for a few seconds. Then Tynan cleared his throat with an 'ahem' and looked over at the gathering below.

'Landau, would you be good enough to bring the kidnapped bride down to us?'

The man obeyed at once, but Tynan stopped him, seeing the blood on his shirt.

'Are you wounded?'

'Just a graze, boss . . . Dillon's first shot.'

'Have Lucia tend to it once you release the girl.'

Reese moved over to check the wounded arm of the one bandit, while Jared told Shane to collect the other. A couple of men carried Waco out of the saloon, and two more removed Dillon. By the time Scarlet appeared, everything was under control.

Jared flew up the stairs, the first of the family to reach Scarlet. They hugged for a few seconds and then she smiled at him.

'I knew you'd come for me.'

'Even the devil himself would have had better sense than to try and stop me,' he said.

She kissed him on the cheek as Lucia

approached to put an arm around her.

'We are so sorry for what Dillon did,' she said. 'I hope you can find someone new to start your life with.'

'Hey!' one of the bandits shouted from below. 'We didn't have no part of any kidnapping.'

'Yeah,' the other joined in. 'What about the rule of everyone protecting everyone in this town?'

'You backed Dillon and Waco's play to overthrow his brother,' one of the gunmen growled. 'You gave up your rights when you made such a poor choice.'

'Besides,' Brett told them, 'you aren't our prisoners. You two are under arrest on the authority of Desiree Moore. She is a Pinkerton agent!'

★ ★ ★

Brett shook hands with Tynan, as Desiree and Scarlet climbed into the Dearborn carriage. Cliff was in the driver's seat of the second buggy with Nessy.

Brett put forth a serious countenance

244

and said, 'I'm sorry about your brother.'

'Kidnapping is a hanging offense,' Jared contradicted from a short way off. 'That mutt was doomed as soon as he grabbed our sister.'

Tynan grimaced. 'I agree.' Then with a frown at Jared, 'And I'm told justice has been served for the rest of the men who were in on that attack . . . except for Landau.'

Brett gave his brother a hard look as well.

'Geez, fellows,' Jared replied, displaying an innocence that would have done a nun proud. 'It seemed uncommonly cruel to drag them three kidnapping murderers several hundred miles in chains, just to be hanged for murder and kidnapping.' He shrugged. 'Besides, each and every one of those jaspers begged me to save them from a long, horrible train ride.'

'Brimstone justice at work,' Tynan approved. 'I'll have some men collect the bodies for burial.'

'Well, I'm glad we worked together to

prevent an all-out war,' Brett spoke to Tynan. 'You have the start of what could be a real town one day, and not just a bandit stronghold.'

Tynan grinned. 'I had to consider your side had — what did you call it — *RJ* and dynamite?'

Brett grinned. 'The first initials of Richard Jordan Gatling. And we needed a couple of equalizers, in case we had to go up against every man-jack in town.'

'I wish you and your family a good trip home,' Tynan said. 'It appears as if Landau is making the journey with you.'

'My sister offered him a job at our ranch. He seems in favor of the idea.'

Tynan stepped back alongside Lucia. She immediately took his arm. Standing together, they appeared to be an ordinary, happy couple.

Brett gave a final wave and mounted his horse. Landau, due to his sore ribs from the gunshot, was driving the ladies' carriage.

The two bandits were tied to their

saddles, with Reb and Dodge keeping watch over them. Shane and Jared rode behind the two carriages. Wyatt took the lead, with Reese and Brett next.

As they rode out of town, Reese spoke to Brett.

'Good thing Tynan was reasonable about fighting us. I can only imagine how many people would have died if we'd had to take on the entire stronghold.'

'He and his wife are trying to make Brimstone a regular town. His biggest problem was not having any control over his brother.'

'Now there's something I can identify with,' Reese teased. 'I swear you and Jared have given me fits since the day you were born.'

'Hey! Jared and Reb are the ones who hanged those three kidnappers.'

He laughed. 'Maybe they really didn't want to ride that train. On our way here, I admit that trying to sleep on those wooden seats was one of the most uncomfortable nights of my life.'

'I didn't mind it at all,' Brett replied. 'Of course, Desiree slept by my side.'

'Speaking of her, I saw the two of you kissing this morning.'

'She was thanking me for helping to capture the two bandits. I believe it might be her last assignment for Pinkerton.'

'Romance is in the air. I noticed that Scarlet and Landau smile a lot at each other, too.'

'Man risked his life to defend her from Dillon, and we're all beholden to him for protecting our sister's virtue.'

'Yeah,' Reese said. 'Maybe I'm reading too much into a look or two.'

'I haven't talked to the man myself, but Scarlet told me he was a decent sort. Said he made a terrible mistake once, but it was understandable.'

'Understandable to a man or to a woman?'

Brett laughed. 'Yes, there's quite a difference between the way a man and a woman think.'

'Back to your future, might I soon

have a new sister-in-law?'

'If we agree to settle down,' Brett admitted. 'What do you think of me becoming your assistant foreman?'

'Shucks, Brett, you've been gone so long, I don't remember if I even like you.'

'Yeah, I don't think I'm cut out to take orders from you, either.'

'How about working in Valeron? The town could use a sheriff.'

'It's a thought. Desiree and me could make a nice home there.'

Reese laughed. 'I reckon you'll end up like most other men. If Desiree decides she is willing to take a chance on you, she will ride herd on you for the rest of your life!'

'Yep,' Brett smiled in return. 'And you know something? That doesn't sound bad at all.'

We do hope that you have enjoyed reading this large print book.

Did you know that all of our titles are available for purchase?

We publish a wide range of high quality large print books including:
Romances, Mysteries, Classics
General Fiction
Non Fiction and Westerns

Special interest titles available in large print are:
The Little Oxford Dictionary
Music Book, Song Book
Hymn Book, Service Book

Also available from us courtesy of Oxford University Press:
Young Readers' Dictionary
(large print edition)
Young Readers' Thesaurus
(large print edition)

For further information or a free brochure, please contact us at:
Ulverscroft Large Print Books Ltd.,
The Green, Bradgate Road, Anstey,
Leicester, LE7 7FU, England.
Tel: (00 44) **0116 236 4325**
Fax: (00 44) **0116 234 0205**